# DANNY ORLIS
## AND THE
# DEFIANT KENT GILBERT

# DANNY ORLIS
## AND THE
# DEFIANT KENT GILBERT

BERNARD PALMER

*Danny Orlis and the Defiant Kent Gilbert*
© 2024 by Bernard Palmer
All rights reserved. First edition 1965.
Second edition 2024.



Scripture quotations from The Authorized (King James) Version. Rights in the Authorized Version in the United Kingdom are vested in the Crown. Reproduced by permission of the Crown's patentee, Cambridge University Press.

*Cover image: Adobe Firefly*

*Character illustrations: John Ball*

*Editor: Jon D. Fogdall*

Aneko Press Youth

www.anekopress.com

Aneko Press, Life Sentence Publishing, and our logos are trademarks of Life Sentence Publishing, Inc.
203 E. Birch Street
P.O. Box 652
Abbotsford, WI 54405

**JUVENILE FICTION / Religious / Christian / Action & Adventure**

Paperback ISBN: 979-8-88936-022-3

eBook ISBN: 979-8-88936-023-0

10  9  8  7  6  5  4  3  2  1

Available where books are sold

# CONTENTS

# CHAPTER 1

# ROOM FOR TWO MORE?

Night stole quietly over the Fairview airport. Danny Orlis checked the mission's Cessna 180 to be sure it was securely tied down, then went to the car where Kay was waiting for him.

"Hi!" he exclaimed, kissing her lightly on the cheek. "How did things go for you today?"

"OK." There was a trace of disappointment in her voice.

"Is everything all right?"

"Of course, Danny. Only I thought we'd hear from the welfare office today. The last time I talked with Mr. Collins he seemed to think they'd have a child for us this week."

"I know." The smile left Danny's young face. "I thought we'd hear from them before this."

Kay Orlis drove away from the airport toward town. "It's so lonesome at home," she said quietly.

Danny nodded. "But we mustn't forget. We committed this entire situation to God, asking Him to work it out as He sees fit. We've got to trust Him."

"I'm sorry, Danny. I know I shouldn't get blue and discouraged."

When they went into the house a few minutes later Jim Morgan was waiting for them. His eyes were sparkling with excitement.

"Boy, am I glad to see you!" he exclaimed. "I thought you'd be home an hour ago."

Danny eyed him questioningly. "What's happened now?"

"Nothing much." Jim shrugged his shoulders. "The phone's just about to ring itself off the wall, that's all. Every time I turn around it starts to ring. I sure have been getting tired of answering it."

Danny laughed. "Now you do have me feeling sorry for you," he said. "But tell us, who's the call for? Kay, or me?"

"Whoever the guy is, he isn't particular," Jim went on. "He asks for either one of you, and I keep telling him you'll be home any time. I tried to give him your cell phone number, but he insists that he wants to talk to you on your landline."

Kay, who had been listening to the conversation, broke in quickly. "Who was it, Jim?"

"I don't know, but you'll find out soon enough. He'll be calling again, any time."

Almost as though that was the signal, the phone rang again. Kay turned and picked up the receiver.

"This is Mr. Collins of the welfare office, Mrs. Orlis," a strange voice said.

"Oh!" Kay caught her breath sharply. "Oh, I see."

"We've been trying to get in touch with you this afternoon."

Holding her hand over the mouthpiece Kay turned excitedly to her young husband. "It's the man from the welfare office."

Danny came over and stood beside the phone.

"We have a boy and a girl for you," the welfare worker said, "if you would like to take them."

"Take them?" Kay echoed. "Of course we'll take them."

There was a short silence.

"We appreciate your willingness, Mrs. Orlis," Mr. Collins went on, "and these children do need a home badly. But before you agree to take them, I would like to tell you something about them. Kent and Jill Gilbert are not ordinary children."

"That doesn't make any difference," Kay broke in. "If they need a home, that's all that matters."

"They do need a home, that's true," he went on, "but they have been neglected and abused until they are unruly, almost delinquent. You may find them very difficult to handle."

Kay was silent momentarily. This wasn't exactly what she and Danny had in mind when they made application to take a child into their home. They had wanted a normal child who needed love and care and the influence of a Christian home.

"I'll talk with Danny about it and let you know a little later," she said.

Kay returned the telephone to its cradle and looked up at her young husband, her eyes shining.

"Oh, Danny!" she exclaimed. "They have a boy and a girl they want us to take."

"How old are they?" he asked.

"I didn't even think to ask." There was a short silence. "Well?"

"Well, what?"

"Are we going to take them?"

Danny laughed.

"Why, Kay," he said, "I thought this was what we had been praying about all summer."

She took a deep breath.

"I know, but–but Mr. Collins says these children are so unruly, they're almost delinquent. He thought we should talk it over before we make up our minds."

Danny went over to the kitchen table and sat down.

"That's something you should answer, Kay," he said. "The biggest job of discipline will be on your shoulders. How about it?" Their eyes met. "Do you feel up to the job?"

Her answer was firm and positive. "As far as I'm concerned, I get the shakes when I think about having to take children like that and be responsible for them. But quiet, well-behaved kids wouldn't need us nearly as much as the two they want us to take."

Danny stood and started for the telephone.

"I agree with you completely," he said, "but I didn't want you to make up your mind because I think it's the thing to do. It's not going to be easy for us to handle them, I'm sure. But with kids like that we'll have an opportunity to really accomplish something."

Neither Danny nor Kay could sleep much that night, and the following morning they were up an hour earlier than usual.

"What time do you suppose Mr. Collins gets down to the welfare office, Danny?" Kay asked, her manner betraying her excitement.

"I don't imagine he'll be there before nine."

They went down to the welfare office shortly after nine o'clock. Mr. Collins was already in his private office.

"I would like to talk with you a little further before you take these children," he said, looking from one to the other. "I told you on the phone last night that they aren't like the average kids in your neighborhood, Mrs. Orlis. We've had a great deal of trouble with them – not only with them, but with their parents."

Danny was the one who spoke.

"What sort of trouble?"

"Morally the parents aren't fit to keep them," he said. "Both Kent and Jill have gone ragged, dirty, and hungry. They've stolen and fought with other kids in the neighborhood. In short, they're problem children, and as long as they remain at home there is no chance for improvement. That is why we instituted court proceedings to take them away from their parents. The judge awarded us custody of the children yesterday. We went out and got them this morning."

Danny nodded. "I see. And how old are they?"

"Kent is thirteen and Jill, the girl, is eleven. They come from a little farm community in the northwest part of the county. They are very intelligent youngsters. In fact, their IQ's are considerably above average. However, neither of them is doing good work in school, and their attendance record is poor. We haven't been able to determine whether that has been due to a lack of interest on the part of the parents, or whether the youngsters have been truant."

Looking over a sheaf of papers, Mr. Collins ticked off the personality traits of the children and outlined the problems that were causing them difficulty. When he finished, Danny looked at Kay.

"They don't sound like prize packages, do they?"

"I don't see how they could be any different than they are," Kay said tenderly. "It certainly doesn't sound as though they have been loved."

"They don't even know the meaning of the word *love*," Mr. Collins broke in. "If these children are taken into a foster home, you can be sure that home is going to experience more than its share of heartaches and problems. Of course, it would be a very rewarding thing if they could be straightened out and made into respectable members of society." He looked from Danny to Kay and back again. "I wouldn't be honest, however, if I didn't acquaint you with the problems as we see them."

The welfare worker took a deep breath, then went on.

"If you would rather wait until the next opportunity to take a child, we would certainly understand. If you feel you want to try in this case but only want to take one youngster, we would be quite willing to separate them and send the other to an orphanage. Frankly, we're at a loss to know what to do with them."

There was a long, tense silence. Kay turned to Danny, at last. "What do you think now, Danny?" she asked. "Are you still willing to try?"

He was a long while in answering.

"I still feel the way I did last night, Kay," he said. "If you're willing to tackle the problem when I'm gone, I'm willing to tackle it while I'm home."

Kay directed her attention to Mr. Collins.

"Could we see the children?" she asked.

He took them through his office and into another across the hall. A boy and a girl – both grimy and unkempt – sat in a corner of the room, their thin, pinched faces solemn. Their clothes looked as though they had not been laundered for a long time, and they had been mended until they were practically patch upon patch. The boy's matted hair was so long it bushed over his ears.

"This is Jill and Kent Gilbert," Mr. Collins said, motioning toward them. He lowered his voice, but not low enough to keep them from hearing. "I'm sorry they're so dirty. I should have had them cleaned up, but my wife's away visiting."

Kent's dark eyes narrowed. "We're just as good as you are!"

"We'll get them cleaned up," Kay said, flashing a friendly smile. Their young faces darkened, however, in response to it.

"Kent and Jill," Mr. Collins said, completing the introduction, "this is Mr. and Mrs. Orlis."

"How are you, Kent?" Danny asked.

The boy surveyed him with hostile, unfriendly eyes. "Do we have to go and live with this old goat?" he demanded belligerently.

Mr. Collins started to protest, but before he could do so Danny spoke up. "I'm not as old as you think I am, Kent."

That seemed to startle the boy. "Well, do we have to live with–with you?" he stammered.

"For a while."

The boy's eyes flashed.

"I'm warnin' you," he snarled, "you ain't goin' to shove me an' Jill around. We ain't takin' nothin' off you or nobody."

Danny ignored his hostility. Kent wouldn't believe him, anyway, if he tried to tell him they weren't going to get "shoved around," as he put it. He and Kay would have to demonstrate it to him.

Kay looked at the little girl. Jill was angular and

bony. Mistreatment had put dark circles under her eyes. She looked as though she had never smiled. At the same time, she was one of the most unattractive children Kay had ever seen. Still her heart went out to Jill. She put out her hand and touched the girl on her tousled head. Jill drew away.

"I'm going to like having you live at our place, Jill," Kay said warmly. "You and I are going to have lots of fun together."

Jill eyed her curiously and without any outward sign of response or affection. Her small body grew rigid.

Kent Gilbert turned fiercely on Kay.

"Keep your dirty mitts off my sister!" he exploded.

"Kent!" Mr. Collins' voice was stern. "That's just about enough out of you, young man. Mr. and Mrs. Orlis want you to go with them. But if you persist in acting this way, I'll have no choice but send you to that children's home in the city. And you've already told me that you don't want to go there."

The boy's eyes blazed.

"We ain't stayin' in no children's home, Buster!" he exploded. "You'd just as well get that in your pointed little head right now. We'll run away first."

Danny read the fright in the boy's eyes. Fright Kent never would have acknowledged.

"Now, Kent," he said quietly, "there's no reason for you to get so belligerent and worked up. Kay and I aren't taking you into our home because we want to hurt you. We'll treat you just as though you belonged to us." He smiled as though to reassure him. "We're taking you because we want to help you."

But Kent Gilbert's manner did not change.

"You can save that kind of talk for somebody who believes it!" His eyes shouted their defiance. "You can't fool me! You're takin' us because the state's payin' you to take us. That's the only reason." The boy's throat choked, and it was a moment before he could speak again. "I'm warnin' you right now that I'm lookin' after Jill. You ain't goin' to get by with treatin' her like she was dirt. I ain't goin' to stand for it."

Danny still did not lose his temper.

"I don't blame you for looking out for your sister, Kent. To tell you the truth, I wouldn't think much of you if you didn't. But there's no use in your standing here trying to argue with me. All I'm going to do is ask that you give us a chance. Come into our home with an open mind and see if we abuse either one of you."

The boy's face clouded.

"I don't see why we can't go back to our own home and live the way we've been livin'. We got by all right."

Mr. Collins turned to Danny. "I think we'd better go over this whole matter in private, Danny, before it goes any further." He guided Danny and Kay back into his office across the hall. "Frankly," he said, "I chose you two for Kent and Jill Gilbert because I felt you were the only ones on our list who were even remotely capable of handling them. But now I'm not at all sure it is possible for anyone to take them and do anything with them."

"They're both scared to death right now."

"They're scared, Danny, but they're still belligerent and overbearing. I don't see how it can work. I'm afraid you are just letting yourself in for a mountain of trouble."

For a moment neither Danny nor Kay spoke.

"I think it would be much better for everybody if those two were placed in an institution right from the start."

Kay shook her head.

"It might be easier for us and for you, Mr. Collins," she said gently, "but we're completely forgetting the kids. What is best for them?"

"We all know what is best for them," the welfare worker said. "But if they don't respond to love and affection, what can we do? How can they be helped?"

"It's going to be hard," Danny said, "but I think Kay and I are both agreed that we should take them."

The welfare worker pursed his lips.

"I've been hoping you would say that," he replied. "I'm sure Kent and Jill will be much better off with you than they ever would be in an institution. Yet I didn't want you to take them without knowing the full story." The corners of his mouth tightened. "As I said, Kent has never had to mind anyone in his entire life. He's not going to like the idea of starting now."

# CHAPTER 2

# AN ENCOUNTER WITH LOVE

**D**anny and Kay Orlis went into the other office with the welfare worker, Mr. Collins. Kent and Jill Gilbert were waiting for them in silence. Kay went over and put her arm about the pitiful little girl's shoulders, smiling as sweetly as she knew how. "You and Kent will be going home with us, Jill," she said. "You're going to be our children for a while." Hesitantly the girl lifted her gaze. Fear still stood in her eyes and darkened her somber face. Her lips quivered uncertainly.

"Do–do you mean we won't have to go to the orphans' home after all?" she asked. "Do you mean we–we're going to get to live in a real house?" Doubt still filled her voice.

Kay hugged her tenderly. "That's right, Jill," she said. "You won't be going to the children's home. You're going to come and live with Danny and me."

There was a brief hesitation. Jill Gilbert looked over at Kent hopefully, as though pleading with him to be happy about the new development, but his expression did not change. Defiantly he stared about the room.

Danny took charge of the situation.

"It's getting late," he said. "I suppose we'd better be going. Where's your suitcase, Kent?"

"Suitcase?" His lips curled bitterly. "Who's got a suitcase? I've got my stuff in that sack, and so has Jill."

Danny and Kay looked down at the tattered paper sack lying on the floor near the doorway.

"Well, get your things, Kent," he said as casually as possible, "and we'll get started for home."

Kent walked along beside him, but winced and drew away when Danny put his hand on his thin shoulder.

Both Danny and Kay tried to talk to the Gilbert youngsters as they drove home, but Kent and Jill only answered with a word or two, if they answered at all. Once in the house, they sat stiffly on the edge of their chairs in the living room, looking about.

Without appearing to stare at them, Kay saw the dirt and grime that had worked deep into the pores of their hands, necks, and faces. Their hair was long and unused to a comb. She turned to Danny.

"In a little while I'll take Jill into the bathroom and help her get cleaned up."

Anger blazed in Kent's eyes, and he faced Danny defiantly.

"You ain't about to give me no bath, mister!" he announced heatedly. "And that's for sure."

Danny laughed good-naturedly.

"Nobody said I was going to Kent," he answered. "You should be able to get clean by yourself."

Kent shook his head.

"You don't listen so good. I ain't takin' no bath, period! You'd just as well forget it."

The young pilot replied quietly, "You'll have to take a bath."

"Who says so?"

"I do." Danny's voice grew firm. "You're going into that bathroom and taking a bath, Kent. And you're going to do it now. If you don't go yourself, I'll take you in there and give you a bath."

The boy did not move.

"You and who else?" he demanded.

Danny took a step toward him, his face stern. Only then did Kent retreat.

"Aw, you don't have to get so shook up about it. I'm goin'."

"That's better."

While Kent was taking his bath Kay laid out some clean underwear of Jim's and found some of Jim's clothes that were too small for him. When Kent finally came into the living room, he looked so different that, except for the shaggy hair, Kay and Danny would have had some difficulty in recognizing him.

"You look like a new boy, Kent," Kay said.

He scowled at her belligerently and turned to Danny.

"I hope you're satisfied."

Kay went in with Jill and helped her bathe and wash her hair. The girl was as dirty as her brother had been to start with, or so it seemed. But the grime wasn't ground into the pores of her skin the way it had been ground into Kent's. And when Kay finally finished, Jill looked almost attractive, except that her face was still thin and bony, and her eyes still mirrored fear. Kay got out some clothes Linda Penner had outgrown and gave them to Jill.

"I'm afraid these are going to be a little large for you, Jill," she explained, "but if you'll wear them now, we'll go uptown and get you some new clothes this afternoon."

The frightened girl eyed her quizzically.

"I could put on my own clothes," she said. "I don't have to wear things that belong to someone else."

Kay did not answer her directly, but with a sudden impulsive gesture she hugged her close.

"You'll never know how glad I am that you're going to live with us, Jill," she said.

The girl was cold and unresponsive. She allowed Kay to show her affection, but she showed none in return.

"Now, I know we won't be going to bed for quite a while, but I'd like to show you your room."

Jill spoke hesitantly. "You are going to let us stay here, aren't you?"

"Of course we are."

There was a moment's silence.

"And–and you won't go away tonight and leave us, will you?" she asked. "After we go to bed and fall asleep, I mean." Fear still tinged her voice.

Kay's face wrinkled questioningly.

"Of course we won't go away and leave you at night. Why would we do that?"

"I don't know." Jill's voice was thin and doubtful, as though she didn't quite believe Kay. "I was just wondering."

After a few minutes Kent and Jill went out on the porch together. Danny and Kay were alone.

"Well, Kay," Danny asked softly, "what do you think of our new family?"

She shook her head.

"I don't know," she answered. "I wish I could tell you. They're both so defiant and afraid." She pursed her lips. "Jill seems to be almost terrified that we will go away tonight after she is in bed. Whatever would give her that idea?"

"Well, the kids were probably left at home plenty of times at night when they were living with their parents. She's probably worrying for fear we are just like them."

"Of course; that's the answer. I'd never thought of that. She's probably awakened in the middle of the night and been terrified to think that her parents were gone, and she and Kent were alone."

Danny's frown deepened.

"They're starved for love, Kay," he said, "but they act as though they are afraid to let us love them."

"It's going to be so hard to break through to them," she said. "They don't respond to anything."

"If we had to look at Kent and Jill from the human point of view, I'm afraid we'd have to give up on them before we start. But the Lord will give us the strength and wisdom we need to help them."

Her smile was confident. "I know that," she said, "but it hurts me so very much to see them resist the love and understanding they need so badly."

Immediately after lunch Danny and Kay took Jill and Kent downtown to get new clothes for them. Jill was as impassive as ever, but Kent was even more arrogant and hostile.

"You ain't doin' this just for us. You're up to something. You can't kid me."

Neither Danny nor Kay answered him.

Once in the store Jill's eyes lit.

"I've been past this store lots of times, Mrs. Orlis," she said, "and I've looked and looked at the dresses in the windows, but I never thought I would ever be able to come in and–and get one."

"We'll get you a school dress and one for Sunday school and church," Kay told her. "Then I'll get some material and make some more dresses for you. I think you should have several, don't you?"

Jill smiled broadly until Kent caught her gaze and frowned. Then she did the same.

Once the shopping was finished, Danny and Kay took them in to get their hair cut.

When Danny and Kay were alone again, Kay turned to her young husband. "Did you see the look on Jill's face when she saw that she was going to get a new dress, Danny? I don't believe she has ever had one before."

"I don't imagine she has. Mr. Collins said they lived in a little shack that most people wouldn't even want to keep cattle in. They hardly had enough to eat, let alone new clothes."

* * *

Jim Morgan was out for the junior high football team that year. After classes were finished for the day, he dashed down to the locker room and changed eagerly into his uniform. For practice he was the first one on the field and the last one off.

Jim wasn't particularly heavy or fast, but what he lacked in natural ability he made up for in drive and determination. He had won for himself the starting slot at center in spite of the fact that two guys who were bigger and speedier than he were also out for the position. He studied the opposition just a little more and scrapped just a little harder than either of the others.

The guys all liked Jim. But after Kent and Jill Gilbert came to live at the Orlis home, they kidded him unmercifully.

"I hear you've got a new brother and a sister, Jim," one of the guys jeered. "Is that right?"

Jim scowled. "What do you mean?"

"Now don't give us that stuff."

Somebody else came up just then. "Let me give you a little advice," he said. "You'd better lock up everything you've got while they're living with you, or that Kent'll have it snitched."

"Is he that kind?"

"You'd better believe it!"

Jim dressed in silence and walked home alone. He went directly to his bedroom and closed the door. Once he was sure that Kent wasn't going to watch him, he took his paper route money from the cardboard box on a shelf in his closet, counted it again to be sure it was all there, and moved it to a new hiding place in his desk behind the bottom drawer. He didn't say anything to Danny about it. Danny probably wouldn't understand why he had to get his money out of the reach of Kent.

During the next few days Kent and Jill seemed to tolerate being at the Orlis home, but that was all. They replied when they were spoken to, but they never said any more than was absolutely necessary. Kent did nothing unless he was specifically told to do it, and then only if there was no possible way of getting out of it. Several times he was late getting home from school. Kay tried to find out where he had been and what he had been doing, but he just gave her a vague answer.

It was the same with homework. He absolutely refused to study at home the way Jim and most of the other kids did. Now and then, Kay talked with him about it, but he passed off her questions belligerently.

"Don't have any homework tonight," he would announce triumphantly. "Got it all done in school."

Kay was not satisfied. "I can't understand that, Kent. Jim has homework nearly every night."

The boy snorted. "That's Jim."

"And when Linda Penner was with us, she nearly always had studies at night."

"Can I help it if they don't study at school and have to take their lessons home at night?" His frown deepened. "Besides, I ain't in the same grade they're in.

Kay talked with Danny about it when he came home from a trip up North.

"Things seem to be going as well as could be expected as far as Kent and Jill are concerned but Kent isn't getting his schoolwork, I'm afraid. I haven't been able to get him to bring any homework home with him."

Danny thought for a moment.

"If I were you, I'd stop by the school as soon as possible, Kay," he suggested. "You can talk with the teachers about Kent and find out what his grades are and just how much homework he should be doing. If he's supposed to be studying at night, we'll have to see that he does it."

"That's not going to be quite as easy as it sounds," she said, concern flickering in her eyes. "I don't think

I have ever felt as helpless as I do when I try to deal with Kent, Danny."

"He's not the easiest boy to handle," Danny admitted.

"I thought Linda was hard, and, in a way, she was. But when I compare her with Kent, I can't see how we thought we had a problem at all. He's so completely unresponsive. When I talk to him, I can't tell whether he's even listening to me or not."

Danny nodded.

"I agree with you completely. Kent and Jill have been permitted to grow up without any parental supervision at all. They don't know what discipline at home is."

# CHAPTER 3

# TROUBLE ON SUNDAY

That evening Jim sat for a long while at the supper table talking with Danny after everyone else had finished eating. Danny had been away for several days, and Jim hadn't had an opportunity to talk with him.

"How's the paper route been going the last couple of weeks, Jim?" Danny asked.

The boy's face crinkled into a smile.

"Things are really looking up. I picked up one new customer last week and two the week before. And I was able to collect a couple of old accounts that I thought were gone."

"That's the way to keep things humming," Danny Orlis told him. "Still thinking about those new skis?"

"I sure am. If I can ever get all the money I have to have, I mean. I just finished saving for the clothes I had to get for this school term, and I've got my tithe paid up. I think I'll be able to get the skis in another month."

Danny nodded his approval.

"That's fine," he said. "You've been paying your own way and saving. I think it's nice that you can get something for yourself."

"I could probably use those old skis for another year," Jim said. "But they're a little short for me, and the sporting goods store downtown has a catalog of some new skis that are really cool. They're just what I want."

Danny got up and poured himself another glass of milk.

"Talking about skis gives me the urge to try it again, Jim," he said. "When you get your new ones, we'll have to go out and give it a try."

"That'd be great. You don't know what you've been missing, Danny. I think I'm beginning to like skiing almost as much as I like fishing."

Kent, who had come into the room a moment before, scowled. "Skiing sounds stupid to me. Who wants to go out in the cold and slide down a hill on a pair of boards? It ain't my idea of fun."

Jim turned to him.

"That's because you haven't done any skiing yourself. Just wait until you try it before you knock it."

Kent grunted scoffingly.

"I'll tell you what we'll do. When I get my new skis, I'll loan you my old pair, and we'll go out and give it a whirl. You won't talk that way after you've tried it a time or two."

The younger boy snorted in derision, stalked into the bedroom, and shut the door.

Jim looked after him quizzically.

"There's one character I can't understand," he said. "What do you suppose is the matter with him? He doesn't act as though he cares about anything or anyone."

Danny shook his head, and it was some time before he spoke. "I wish I knew, Jim," he said slowly. "I certainly wish I knew."

The boy took a deep breath.

"When I first came to live with Uncle Carl, Aunt Mary, and you, I know I was disagreeable and hard to get along with, but I don't think I was as bad as he is. It doesn't make any difference what you try to do for that guy, he's still ugly." Danny laughed.

"You gave Mother and Dad their share of headaches. I can tell you that."

"And I've felt awfully bad about it, too."

The youthful missionary pilot breathed deeply.

"They have been repaid for any trouble you've caused them, Jim," he replied, "by seeing you come through for the Lord Jesus the way you have. I'd be happy if Kent and Jill would make half the progress you have made, in regard to spiritual things."

Jim Morgan pushed back from the table.

"The thing that bothers me the most is the way he treats our whole family, Danny. I don't think he's said half a dozen decent words to any of us since he and Jill came here to live. He acts as though we, and everyone else in town, have it in for him. He acts as though he's got to watch us as closely as he can or we're going to take advantage of him."

Danny leaned back and crossed his legs.

"Well, Jim, if you had been treated the way Kent Gilbert's parents have treated him, I imagine you'd have trouble trusting anyone too. Those kids haven't had it easy at home. That's for sure."

"You'd think that would be all the more reason why he would appreciate what you and Kay are trying to do for Jill and him," Jim went on. "You're taking them into the house and treating them like members of the family. But that doesn't seem to faze him at all. He still thinks you've got some ulterior motive for being nice to them."

Kay came into the kitchen and pulled up a chair.

"And just what is this big discussion all about?" she asked.

"I was just telling Danny what I think about Kent," Jim said.

Danny sipped his milk thoughtfully. "It's our responsibility to show Kent that we love his sister and him. Somehow, we've got to make him understand that we are nice to him because we love him. I think he'll respond when we can make him see that."

Jim shook his head, and doubt stood in his young eyes.

"I wish I could be as sure of that as you are," he said. "I don't believe Kent will ever appreciate anything anybody does for him."

For the space of a minute or two no one spoke. Danny had the disturbing suspicion that Jim was right. Kent didn't act as though he would ever appreciate anything that was done for him.

The first Sunday Kent and Jill were with the Orlis family, there was a stiff argument as to whether the two of them would go to Sunday school or not. Danny had taken it for granted that they would go and had said nothing to them about it until nine o'clock Sunday morning when he went in to wake Kent. The boy rolled over sleepily, rubbing his eyes.

"What's the big idea?" he muttered. "This is Sunday, ain't it?"

Danny smiled good-naturedly. "This is Sunday. That's the reason I came in to wake you. You're going to have to hurry in order to get to Sunday school and church."

Kent sat up quickly, defiance blazing in his eyes.

"Sunday school and church?" he repeated. "Who said I was goin'?"

Danny's gaze met his evenly.

"We always go to Sunday school here, Kent. Sunday is the most important day of the week, and church and Sunday school are the most important places we go.

"That stuff may be all right for you, but me and Jill ain't havin' any of it."

"You and Jill have never been to Sunday school, Kent," Danny said. "After you go today, you'll know what it's like. You'll enjoy it, all right. Everybody does."

"Not us! You're just wastin' your breath, Danny," Kent countered. "I said we ain't goin' to no Sunday school or church, and we ain't. That's all there is to it." He rolled over and closed his eyes.

"Kent," Danny said with a firmness he had never before used on the boy, "I told you it's time to get up, and that's just what you're going to do. Get out of bed and get dressed for Sunday school. And don't let me have to tell you again, or it will be unpleasant for both of us."

For the space of a minute Kent stared at Danny trying to decide just how far he could go with him. Apparently, he realized he had pushed as hard and as far as he could. Eyes blazing, he got out of bed.

"I think I should've let 'em put me in that orphanage," he muttered. "This is worse than a jail!"

Danny waited until he was sure Kent was following orders. Then he went into the other room where Kay was reading over her Sunday school lesson one last time. They heard Kent grumbling to himself but said nothing to show they had.

At last Kent stormed into the kitchen, his shoes in his hand.

"The shoe polish is in the bathroom, Kent," Kay said, "if you want to polish your shoes."

"That's all I hear around here," he exploded. "Eat your cereal. Polish your shoes. Brush your teeth. Do you know what this place is like? A jail!"

Jim snickered and looked down quickly.

"You'd think a guy could do what he wants to do once in a while," he went on. "When we were home, we could stay in bed all day Sunday if we wanted to."

Jill came out at that moment in her new dress.

"Good morning, Jill."

The thin-faced girl was frowning. "I can't comb my hair."

"Come over here, honey, and I'll help you." Kay combed her hair and pinned it in place with a pert bow. She straightened her stockings and smoothed the ties on her dress. When she finished, she looked down at the pathetic little girl with the sad, unsmiling eyes.

"My, but you look sweet, Jill."

The girl's expression did not change, but by this time Kay had learned not to expect it to change. She put an arm about Jill's frail shoulders and hugged her affectionately.

In a moment or two Danny came striding in.

"It looks as though everybody is ready in here," he said. "Let's get our coats and get on our way. We don't want to be late."

Jill's lips trembled, and fear filled her eyes.

"Do–do I have to go, Kay?"

Kay knew just how Jill felt. Sunday school and church were something new, a strange place where she had never been before. And her brother was set against going. It was small wonder that she was afraid.

"You'll like it in Sunday school and church, Jill," Kay told her, quietly. "Everybody will be nice to you.

After you've been there once, you'll find out that it's one of the nicest places you've ever gone."

"Will–will I be able to sit with you?"

Kay shook her head.

"I'd like to have you sit with me," she said, "but we divide into different classes. And besides, Danny and I each teach a class."

"Then I won't go," she announced defiantly. "I'll stay at home!"

"You wouldn't want to be with us, anyway," Kay said. "You'd want to be with children of your own age."

"But I don't want to be with the kids my own age," Jill retorted. "They all laugh at me and–and make fun of me at school. I don't want to be with them."

Kay's smile was sympathetic and understanding.

"I'm sure that makes you feel bad," she went on, "but you won't have to worry about the children at. Sunday school making fun of you."

A question gleamed in the girl's eyes.

"Are you sure?"

I'm positive."

Kent came into the room, still scowling his displeasure.

"If we've got to go to Sunday school," he blurted, "I guess we've got to go. But that don't mean we've got to like it."

He made no further protest about going to church. When the services were over, he did not comment, and nobody asked him about it. Kay talked with Jill, however, to find out if she liked the services.

"It was all right, I guess." She smiled uncertainly. "And–and nobody made fun of me."

"I knew they wouldn't. Everyone was so glad to see you, they wouldn't say anything. Besides, they won't even *think* anything bad about you."

Kent was bold and hostile. "Go ahead and ask me how I liked church," he demanded. "Go ahead and see what sort of an answer you get. I dare you."

Danny drove into the yard and stopped. He and Kay went into the house and Jill followed, leaving Jim and Kent alone. Kent stared after them, anger flaming in his eyes.

"The old goat!" Kent snapped disrespectfully. "Making me go to church! I hope he chokes!"

For an instant anger smoked across Jim's vision. He clenched his fists until his knuckles showed white.

"Just who're you calling an old goat?" His voice was trembling.

"I'll give you three guesses, wise guy!"

Jim pressed close to him and stared straight into his eyes.

"I've just about had it, Kent," he warned ominously. "Ever since you've come here you've been stepping on somebody's toes. You can't talk about Danny Orlis like that and get away with it."

"Who says I can't?"

"I say so. He's one of the nicest guys you've ever met in all your life. And if you'll give him half a chance, he'll be a friend of yours."

Kent faced Jim, his legs spread wide, and his young jaw set. When he spoke, his lips curled contemptuously.

"I'll call him anything I want, and you can't stop me!

Jim cocked his fist. Anger caused his lithe body to tremble.

"Now get this and get it straight! If I hear you make one more crack about Danny or Kay either one, you've got to answer to me! Do you understand that?"

At that moment Kay came to the kitchen door and called to them.

Jim glanced over his shoulder. "We'll be right there."

There was a short, taut silence. Jim lowered his voice to a whisper.

"I'm warning you for the last time, Kent. Don't you go around talking about Danny or Kay. If you do, you'll get into real trouble!"

Face flushed, Kent whirled and stalked into the house. He sat at the table that noon, staring down at his plate and eating very little. As soon as they finished, he went to his room and closed the door.

Danny noticed it.

"Now, what's the matter with him?" he asked.

"Don't worry about him," Jim replied without looking up. "He'll be all right."

"Jim," Danny said suspiciously, "did you and Kent have some trouble?"

"No trouble. I just straightened him out on a few things, that's all."

# CHAPTER 4

# THE WRONG CROWD

Jim Morgan continued to hold his post as center in the junior high starting lineup. He played well enough on offense to stay in most of the time when Fairview had the ball, but defense was his specialty. As the season wore on, he learned to diagnose the opposition's plays with surprising regularity. He found it easier for him, at least, to stand back of the line a step, surveying the situation until an instant before the ball was snapped. And, more often than not, as the play unfolded, he drove straight for the ball carrier with uncanny accuracy.

Usually, the fans at Fairview followed only the senior high squad, but this year the junior high eleven won their games so well that quite a number of people could be found in the stands the afternoons they played, especially when they met Westerville.

Jim started the Westerville game as he always did,

but from the first play after the visitors returned the kickoff it was obvious that he was turning in his best game of the season. He knifed through the Westerville line and nailed the ball carrier for a nine-yard loss. On the next play he knocked down a short pass as the receiver was about to tuck it under his arm. Westerville kicked on fourth down, but Jim almost blocked the kick.

As they trotted down the field to begin the second quarter, the left guard turned to Jim.

"I wonder if that sportswriter who picked Westerville to skin us by three touchdowns is here this afternoon. If he is, he's getting his eyes full."

"The game's not over yet," Jim reminded him.

"No," the guard said, "but the way you've been slamming into their offense and scrambling their plays I think we can hold them scoreless."

Jim shook his head doubtfully.

"I'd settle for a win by one point."

At half time Fairview led fourteen to nothing, and when the final gun sounded they had shut out Westerville with a resounding thirty-four to nothing victory.

Walking to the bus, Jim grinned happily. He had always wondered what it would feel like to turn in a top game. Now he knew. Several people stopped and congratulated him. After a local businessman left his side, he looked around and saw Linda Penner.

"Hi, Jim," she said. Her voice was warm and friendly.

"Hello, Linda. I didn't even know you were here."

"I don't usually come to the junior high games," she said, "but I'm so glad I got to see this one. You certainly were the star."

Jim flushed. "The next time I play I'll probably fall flat on my face."

Some of the guys were slow in getting to the bus. While Jim waited, he and Linda stood there, visiting.

"How are things at home, Jim?" she asked.

A frown crossed his young face.

"All right, I guess. At least they would be all right if that Kent Gilbert wasn't such a loser."

There was a brief silence.

"I don't know whether you know it or not," Linda went on guardedly, "but he's been hanging around with Jack Ross."

"Jack Ross!" Jim caught his breath. "Kent's younger than I am, and Jack Ross is a lot older than I am. What on earth could they be doing running around together?"

Linda shook her head.

"I don't know why they would be together," she replied, "but I know they are. I saw them together yesterday afternoon."

The corners of Jim's mouth tightened.

"The kind of a guy Jack Ross is, that sure isn't good."

Jim was quiet and preoccupied on the bus ride back to the high school where he and his teammates showered and dressed. He didn't know why it bothered him so much that Kent was running around with Jack Ross, but it did. Jack wasn't the sort of a guy any decent guy would care to be with – especially someone so much younger. Danny should know about this right away so he could put a stop to it.

Jim hadn't planned on saying anything to Kent about it, but Kent mentioned it to him as soon as he got home. Kent was in the living room alone when Jim entered after the game.

"How'd the game turn out this afternoon?" Kent asked.

"All right." Jim went over and sat down near the window. "We knocked off Westerville thirty-four to nothing." His eyes narrowed. "I thought you said you were going to be there."

"I did plan on it, but I–I had something else to do." A wide grin crossed his face.

"It looks as though it must have been important."
"It was important. You should've been with me." Jim's forehead knitted curiously. "And just where did you go that was so exciting that you'd miss a good football game for it?"

"A friend of mine gave me a ride in his hot rod," Kent said, a superior little smile toying with the corners of his mouth. "And did we ever blast off! I'd give *anything* to have a car like that."

Jim's eyes narrowed. "This friend of yours wouldn't happen to be Jack Ross, would it?" he asked.

A queer look darkened Kent's face.

"How did you know?" he demanded.

"Oh, I get around."

"Jack's got the slickest hot rod in the country." Kent's voice raised defensively. "You should see the way he's got that job souped up. If he'd put wings on her, she'd fly."

Jim Morgan replied laconically. "That car of his goes so fast he's been picked up two or three times for speeding. About once more and he's had it. He'll lose his driver's license."

"Jack told me about that," Kent answered. "He said the cops've got it in for him because his car'll do so much more than theirs will. That's why they've picked him up. But if he wanted to, he could go off and leave them like they were standing still."

For a brief space of time Jim did not speak.

"Jack's going to start entering his car in some of the hot rod races around Fairview," Kent continued. "He's going to take me with him to help."

"How come you're such good friends with Jack Ross all of a sudden?"

"I've been helping him with his car," Kent said. "And he's been promising to give me a ride. So today he came over to school and picked me up and everything. And, was it ever cool! You should take a ride in that car, Jim. It really goes."

Jim Morgan nodded.

"If you'd like to go for a ride sometime, I think I could fix it up for you," the younger boy went on. "Jack said he'd give some of my friends a ride someday."

"No, thank you," Jim said. "The way Jack drives I wouldn't care to ride with him. And even if I did want to, I just wouldn't care to run around with him."

Kent bristled quickly.

"What's wrong with Jack?" he demanded. "Answer me that."

Jim leaned forward earnestly. "I've been wanting to talk to you about him, Kent. He isn't the sort of a guy you should run around with."

Indignation flashed haughtily in the younger boy's eyes.

"And just why not?" he asked. "How do you know the kind of a guy I should run around with? Just because he doesn't go to that stupid church of yours, you think he's about ready for the penitentiary or something. Well, I can tell you one thing, Jack's just as good as you are! And I'm going to run around with him all I want to! Neither you nor anybody else can stop me!"

"You don't know the guy like I do, Kent," Jim went on. "Sure, he looks like a big hero to you. He's got this expensive hot rod and plenty of spending money. He can make himself out to be a big shot. He fools a lot of kids."

"You're just jealous, that's all."

"I'm not jealous of Jack Ross. He's been arrested a couple or three times for speeding, and they've suspected him of some more serious things they haven't been able to prove. If you run around with a guy like that, you might get into real trouble."

"Says you!"

Jim sighed.

"I–I've never told anyone else in Fairview this, Kent," he began, "but I want you to see that I know what I'm talking about when I warn you about Jack. Before I came to live with Danny's parents at Angle Inlet, I got in with the wrong crowd and got into real trouble. The judge sent me to live with the Orlis family instead of sending me to a boys' reformatory. Even then I didn't learn my lesson, and I got into some more trouble after I came to their place. Both times it was because I got in with older guys who pretended to be such good friends of mine."

A queer look came into Kent's face.

"Are you giving me the straight goods?" he asked.

"You can check with Danny if you want to," Jim replied. "I'm telling you I know what I'm talking about. That's why I hate to see you running around with a character who can get you into trouble."

Kent took a long breath. "I don't want to get in a jam with the cops, but…."

"Then you'd better leave Jack alone. He's bad medicine."

Although it seemed that the younger boy was not going to run with Jack anymore, Jim told Danny about it.

"I'm glad you had a talk with him, Jim," Danny said. "That might do a lot more good than it would for me to say anything to him. But I'll talk with him about it myself as soon as I get the chance. We can't let him start running around with someone who will be a bad influence on him."

Jim went into his bedroom and came out a minute or two later with a colored folder on ski equipment.

"I went down to the sporting goods store at noon today, Danny, and picked this up. I'm almost ready to order those new skis, and I'd like to get your opinion of the pair that would be best for me."

Danny took the folder. "Now, which pair are you considering?"

Jim pointed them out to him. Danny read the description and studied the illustration. "They look good to me, Jim," he replied, "and not a bad price for good, serviceable skis, either."

The boy beamed. "I'll stop in the sporting goods store on the way to school tomorrow and have Mr. Anderson order them for me."

Danny wanted to have a chance to talk with Kent about Jack Ross that evening, but he was not able to do so. Kent had already gone to bed by the time Danny was free. The young pilot had to fly up North for several days, and it was the first of the week before he was able to see Kent alone.

"I haven't been running around with Jack Ross," Kent said blandly. "Whoever told you that lied to you."

Danny spoke quickly.

"I wasn't lied to," he retorted. "Jim told me you had gone for a ride with Jack in his hot rod, Kent. And Jim doesn't lie."

"Oh, that." Kent managed a queer little laugh. "I thought you meant I had gone for a ride with Jack after Jim talked with me. When he told me the kind of a guy Jack Ross is, I thought I'd better drop him. So I did."

"I'm glad to hear that," Danny said. "Jack is several years older than you are. It's never good to run around with older boys. And he isn't the right sort of person to be with anyway. He would just mean trouble."

"You don't have to worry about me, Danny," Kent assured him. "As soon as Jim told me the kind of a guy Jack is, I decided right away that I didn't want to be around him."

"That's fine, Kent," the missionary pilot said. "And I'm so glad you decided that on your own."

Neither Kent nor Danny noticed that Jill was sitting quietly in the room. She did not speak until after Danny had left. Then she fastened her big dark eyes on her brother's face somberly.

"Kent," she said, "you didn't tell Mr. Orbs the truth."

Fear leaped to his face.

"What do you mean?"

"You were riding in that Jack Ross' car this afternoon after school," she announced.

"How do you know?"

"I saw you with him. I saw him stop his car in front of the school, and you came running out and climbed in. Then he drove off."

"That was somebody else," Kent said. "That wasn't the boy Danny was talking about."

But Jill stood her ground.

"It was, too, the boy Mr. Orlis was talking about," she continued. "You called him Jack. And it's the same boy I've seen you with several times lately." Her voice rose accusingly. "You didn't tell Mr. Orlis the truth."

Kent looked about quickly, to be sure nobody had overheard them.

"Jill," he whispered, "don't say anything to Danny or anyone else about seeing me with Jack, will you? If you do tell anyone about it. I'll be in terrible trouble."

"But–."

"I might even have to go to that orphanage," he said, "and leave you here with Mr. and Mrs. Orlis all alone. And if that happened, they'd probably be so mad they'd make you work hard and everything. They might even make you stay out of school and clean the house."

He grasped her by the shoulders with both hands.

"You aren't going to say anything to anyone about it, are you?"

Eyes wide with fear, she shook her head.

"I–I won't tell anyone, Kent," she said. "I won't say anything to anyone about it."

"Cross your heart?"

"Cross my heart."

He relaxed.

"Good. I knew I could depend on you." He smiled broadly. "You and I have got to stick together, Jill. I won't tell anything I know about you, and you won't tell anything you know about me. OK?"

Jill nodded uncertainly.

# HOOKY FOR A DAY

The following Sunday morning Kent surprised Danny, Kay, and Jim by making no protest about going to church. He got up without being called, dressed, and shined his shoes before breakfast. "Kent," Danny said, "you've showed us all up this morning. You make me ashamed of myself for being so slow."

Kent grinned. "If I have to go to Sunday school and church, I guess the least I can do is to be ready so we can be there on time."

Kay nodded vigorously.

"That's just the way I feel," she said. "But I do have to admit that neither Danny nor Jim is bad about poking around on Sunday morning. I think we're in Sunday school early almost every Sunday."

They went to Sunday school at the regular time that morning and stayed for church as usual. Jim sat behind Kent.

He couldn't help noticing that Kent was strangely moved by the things the pastor said. He clung to every word of the challenging message. Although an invitation wasn't given often on Sunday morning, that day was an exception. Kent squirmed as the pastor asked anyone who wished to accept Christ as his Savior to step forward. It looked as though Kent was almost persuaded to take a stand for Christ.

Jim prayed quietly for him, but Kent's shoulders squared, and he did not move until after the benediction. Then he marched out without looking in either direction.

Jim told Danny and Kay about it at the first opportunity, and they were as pleased as he was. Danny's smile was broad.

"That is good news," he said. "If we can just reach Kent for the Lord, I think most of our troubles with him will be over."

"If he consecrates his life to Christ," Kay added.

"I guess that's what I should have said. If–if we can reach him for the Lord, it won't be too difficult to get hold of Jill," Danny went on. "She seems to be very anxious to do everything that he does."

"That's right. And I only hope it is soon – for Kent's sake," Kay said.

"I feel exactly the same way. But, you know, it is good to hear that he's been touched by the gospel. It shows that he's not as hard as he'd like to make us think he is."

Kay's voice grew even more serious. "We'll have to keep on praying for him. He needs the Lord as much as anyone I have ever known."

The following day Danny had to fly to Minneapolis to pick up a missionary. He wanted Kay to go along, but she declined saying, "I'd like to go with you, Danny, but with Kent and Jill here and as difficult as they are to handle, I think it would be better if I stayed home. It's hard to know what they might do, even if we were gone for just a couple of days."

"I suppose you're right," he said, "but I miss being able to take you with me once in a while."

"And I miss going too."

Danny left fairly early in the morning. Kay got the children off to school and was just finishing her housework shortly before noon when the telephone rang.

"This is Miss Thompson, the principal at Madison Grade School," the voice on the phone said. "Is this Mrs. Orlis?"

"Yes."

"Are you the couple who are taking care of Kent Gilbert and his sister?"

"That's right," Kay said. "Is–is there something wrong?"

"We're just making a routine check to see why Kent isn't in school today. Is he ill?"

Kay gasped.

"Isn't he in school?" she echoed. "He left here this morning at the same time he always does."

Kay pressed **End**, slowly put her phone down, and went over to the window and looked out. It was a gray afternoon, and there was a touch of snow in the air. It looked as though it was going to get decidedly colder. But the chill of the weather was nothing compared to the chill within her heart.

Since Jim Morgan had come to live with them, he had not always obeyed by any means. They had had to deal with him, and on occasion they had had to punish him. But there was an openness about the things Jim did. When Danny had talked to him, he had made no effort to deceive, even though he knew he would be punished.

Linda Penner had been a bit worse when it came to lying to them. But she was nothing like Kent Gilbert. Kent was "slick" in his deception, and he had a certain cunning that helped him contrive to get his own way. He wriggled, squirmed, and twisted. Whatever he did made no difference to him, as long as he got his own way.

Now this had happened, and Danny was not home to handle the situation. Impulsively Kay picked up her phone, started to dial a number, and stopped. Then she went into the bedroom and knelt in prayer.

Somehow, she got through the afternoon.

There was no word from Kent, or about him, but an hour after the usual time for him to come home he showed up. He came into the house through the back door and headed for the bathroom to wash up when Kay heard him.

"Kent," she called, "is that you?"

"Yeah, I'm here." There was belligerence in his young voice.

Kay came to the hall and eyed him coldly. "Where have you been?" she demanded.

"Just around," he said evasively.

As he spoke, she saw that his shirt and trousers were dirty and torn.

"Kent!" Kay exclaimed, "whatever happened to your clothes?"

Sheepishly he looked down.

"I–I guess I did get them a little dirty."

"I guess you did!" Her temper exploded. "You look as though you've been rolling around in grease. The front of your shirt's torn, and one knee of your trousers is split out. What have you been doing?"

Kent paused, but there was no hesitation in his voice when he began to speak.

"Well, it's this way. I was coming home from school when I saw an old man who had a flat tire. He didn't think he could change it himself, so he said he'd give me fifty cents to help him. I didn't know his jack and lug wrench were so dirty."

Kay opened her mouth to retort hotly but stopped herself.

"Go on and get washed up," she told him. "You'll have to change clothes before you come to supper."

His mouth tightened.

"There ain't no call for you to get so mad and

blow your stack. All I did was stop and help an old man change a tire."

"We'll talk with you about it later."

Kay didn't feel that she could cope with the situation herself. She would have to wait until Danny got home.

That evening as soon as supper was over Kent went to his room. Jill followed him.

"Kent," she said, her eyes accusing him, "you weren't in school today."

He frowned. "Now who told you that?"

"I heard some of the bigger boys talking. They said you hadn't come to school because you were–were playing hooky."

His voice lowered.

"But you ain't goin' to tell on me, are you?"

She shook her head uncertainly.

"You shouldn't play hooky, Kent," she continued. "You'll get in bad trouble. Maybe they'll even expel you."

"Nobody's goin' to know about it," he said, eyeing her obliquely. "That is, if you don't squeal on me."

"I–I told you I wouldn't."

"Good." Relief reflected in his eyes. "We ain't goin' to tell anybody anything about each other, are we?"

She shook her head.

"To show you I trust you, I'll tell you where I was," he said. "I was almost at school this morning when Jack Ross came along and asked me to help him work on his car. So that's what I did."

"You shouldn't do things like that, Kent. You'll get in trouble."

"A guy's got to help a friend when he gets the chance, especially a great friend like Jack."

Kay didn't know how Kent got back into school the next morning without a note from her, but somehow, he managed. That evening Danny returned, and, as soon as Kent got home, he called the boy into his study.

"Kent," he said. "I'm not going to ask you if you were in school yesterday because I don't want to tempt you to tell me something that isn't true. Miss Thompson, the principal at your school, called and told Kay you were absent yesterday. And you weren't sick."

Fear and anger mingled in the boy's eyes.

"So what?" he demanded defensively.

"Would you care to tell me why you skipped school?" Danny asked.

"You know so much. Why don't you tell me?"

The line about Danny's mouth deepened. "We're going to ground you for two weeks, Kent."

"What do you mean?"

"You are to go nowhere except to school and church. The rest of the time you will be home. And if you play hooky again, you'll spend a month at home."

Kent gasped. "What?"

"I think you heard me very well, Kent," Danny replied evenly. "You are to spend two weeks at home except for going to school and church."

"Just for skipping school one day?" Kent demanded.

"I'm afraid you don't realize just how serious this matter is. You're setting up a pattern of truancy and deceit that is going to cause you trouble all the rest of your life, to say nothing of ruining your education."

Kent fell silent.

"And there is another matter I think we need to talk about," Danny continued. "You ruined the new trousers and shirt we bought you. We'll have to take you to town tomorrow and get more for you."

The boy scowled. "I ain't kickin' about the way they look, am I?"

"No, but you can't go to school that way."

Kent shrugged with exaggerated indifference. "Suit yourself. It's your money that's paying for them."

"That's right. I'm paying for them. But it's only going to be a loan to you, Kent. I'm going to expect you to rake leaves and scoop snow to pay back what the clothes cost us. You will have to give us half the money you earn until you've paid back what we spend on you tomorrow."

Anger flushed Kent's face.

"If I have to pay for them, I should be able to decide whether I get them or not!"

* * *

It was strange how different the school year had been for Linda Penner as compared to the year before. She had been studying so hard she had found little time for dates and social activities. She went to the young people's parties at church and to some of the school parties; however, she had not even seen Jack Ross to talk to him for several weeks. She was surprised when he stopped her in the hall to talk to her one afternoon. She was even more surprised at the glow of satisfaction she felt at being singled out by him. She hadn't even known he still meant something to her. For a moment she found herself pleased that he had failed so many of his classes the year before and that he had to return to take his senior year over again.

Jack came swaggering up to her as she was getting her coat from her locker. A grin lit his handsome face.

"Hello, kitten," he said. "Long time, no see."

She looked up. "Why hello, Jack. How are you?"

The corners of his mouth drooped.

"You'll never know how lonesome I am. I cry myself to sleep every night."

Linda laughed. "Now that is too bad. And what's causing that, Jack?"

"Something sad happened to me." There was mockery in his voice. "You see, my girl went religious on me, and now she thinks she's too good for me."

Linda colored. "Jack!"

"Well, it's the truth," he said. "She thinks she's so much better than I am that she's not going to go with me any-more. She won't even let me take her home from school."

"You know that's not true!" She spoke guardedly.

"That's the way I get it," he went on. "She says any guy she goes with has got to be a religious fanatic just like she is. So, I'm lonesome – crying myself to sleep every night."

Linda bristled.

"Jack," she said, "if you keep talking that way, I'm going home. I'm not even going to stand here and talk with you."

"See," he retorted, "that's just what I mean. But let me clue you in, Linda. You should stick around. There's an outside chance that you'll be able to convert me. Did you ever think of that?"

She did not answer him.

"It's sure too bad that you and I aren't going steady now. We'd really be having ourselves a time."

Her expression did not change, but a new expectation leaped within her. True, Jack was wild. He wasn't the sort of guy a Christian girl should be dating, but they had had real fun together. There was no getting around that. More than once she had thought about the good times she had had when she was with him.

"Remember how much fun we used to have going out in my hot rod and burning up the road?" he asked.

Linda shivered.

"Fun?" she echoed. "I was terrified."

"You can't kid me. You used to have as much fun as I did."

"Well–." Her voice died away.

"Until you got to be such a religious fanatic that you thought it was a sin to go out with me." He paused momentarily. "I mean it, Linda. The worst thing that ever happened to you was when you got religion. Nobody's been able to have any fun with you since…. You're a square!"

Linda hesitated. She knew that wasn't quite true. She had more friends now as a Christian than she had ever had before. The only thing was that her new friends didn't count for anything with Jack because they didn't do the same things he did.

"I wish you'd go to church and Sunday school, Jack," she told him. "If you'd only go a few times to see what it's like, I'm sure you'd feel the way I do. You'd want to go whether I asked you to or not."

He laughed boisterously.

"You'd just as well save your breath, kitten. I'm gettin' along just fine the way things are. If you had your way, you'd make as big a fanatic out of me as you are, and I'm not going to let you. I'm going to have fun. I'm going to live it up!"

There was a short silence. Then Jack lowered his voice and said, "I'm going to make a little prediction, Linda. One of these days when you see how things are going with me, you're going to be mighty sorry you let that religion of yours bust us up."

Curiosity gleamed in her eyes. "What makes you say that?" she asked.

"I've got a little deal cooking."

"What kind of a deal?"

"Wouldn't you like to know?" He grinned at her impishly. "Just wouldn't you like to know?"

There was a dull ache in Linda's heart as Jack walked arrogantly down the hall and out into the sharp, early-winter afternoon.

# CHAPTER 6

# KENT'S "WAGES"

The two weeks that Kent Gilbert was to remain at home dragged by endlessly for him. He complained about it bitterly to anyone who would listen, but Danny did not relent. It was not until Kent had spent fourteen days of restricted activity that he was permitted to go other places again. Even then, Danny talked with him first.

"You're free to go out now, Kent," he said, "as long as we give you permission to go and as long as we know exactly where you are going and when you are going to be home."

Kent grunted unintelligibly. When Danny was gone, Kent turned to Jim. "Having to stay home for two solid weeks!" he exclaimed. "I feel like I just got out of jail."

Jim's eyes met his evenly.

"I imagine that's just the way Danny wanted you to feel," he said. "And I can tell you this much – if you play hooky again, you'll really be in trouble. You can't fool around with Danny. I know. I tried it."

"If he thinks he's going to get anywhere with that sort of stuff, he's crazy. Anytime I want to play hooky I'll play hooky. It ain't goin' to make no difference to me what Danny Orlis thinks about it."

Jim shrugged indifferently. "Well, don't say I didn't warn you. If you get into a real jam with Danny, it's your neck, not mine."

The following Saturday afternoon Kent was gone. Just before supper that night he came swaggering in and stood before the missionary pilot.

"Danny," he asked, "how much did you say I owed you for those clothes?"

Danny pursed his lips thoughtfully.

"Kay has the bills, and I can't remember just how much they cost. As I recall, they were eleven or twelve dollars."

"Well," Kent said arrogantly, "figure it up."

"I don't think there's any point in getting the exact amount now. You won't be able to pay for them yet."

Kent sat down and crossed his legs. A superior little smile tugged at the corners of his mouth.

"What makes you think I won't?" he demanded. "If you'll tell me how much I owe you, I'll give you the money, so I won't have you holding that over me."

Danny hoped his face did not show the surprise he felt.

"Just a minute, Kent," he said. "I'll get the bill

from Kay." He was back in a minute or two. "You owe us $10.98." The boy took the bill and scanned it as though to check the accuracy of the items. "Here you are. Got change for $15.00?"

Danny's gaze sought his and held it forcibly.

"Now where did you get fifteen dollars, Kent?" he asked.

"What difference does it make to you where I got it?" Kent asked haughtily. "You're gettin' your money. That's what you've been howlin' about, ain't it?"

"Not exactly. I insisted that you pay for those clothes so that you'll take care of them. Sometimes a guy is awfully careless with things that don't cost him anything." He paused. "But even more important than that is the way you got the money."

"Let's skip the lecture!"

"I can't let you talk to me that way, Kent," Danny said firmly. "And as for the money, I've got to know where it came from."

"Why? Give me one good reason."

"I want to be sure you got it honestly."

Kent's manner changed perceptibly.

"Well, I got the money honestly," he replied. "You won't have to worry about that."

"Where did you get it?"

The boy's proud lips curled.

"I got a job helping a guy."

"And just whom did you help?"

"A guy. That's all."

Danny questioned him quietly but with an insistence that probed deep for answers.

"What were you doing for him?"

Kent jumped to his feet.

"For cryin' out loud!" he snorted. "I went out and got the job because I tore those clothes you bought me, and you said you were going to make me pay for them. Then, when I bring you the money, you won't take it before you give me the third degree! I'm about fed up!"

Kent stormed into the other room.

Danny stared after him in bewilderment.

It was several minutes later that Kay came into the room where Danny was sitting. She read the troubled look in his eyes. "Is there something wrong, Danny?"

"I don't know," he said slowly. "Kent just tried to repay the money we spent for his new trousers and shirt."

"Where would he get that much money so soon?" she asked.

"That's what bothers me," he replied. "I don't have the slightest idea where it came from, or what he did to earn it – if he did earn it."

"Oh, Danny!" Concern flickered in her eyes. "You don't think he got it some other way, do you?"

"I would like to think he had earned the money honestly, Kay, but I don't see how he could have. Today is the only time he'd actually have been able to work. We've kept him at home the past two weeks, so he couldn't have earned any money then even if he had

had a job." Danny paused momentarily. "A boy just couldn't earn fifteen dollars in one day of working."

There was a brief silence.

"The thing that bothers me the most is that we don't have any way of finding out the truth unless he tells us. And from talking to him I don't think he's going to tell us much."

Kay nodded. "That's the way I feel. It doesn't seem likely that he would be able to earn so much money in such a short time. But we can't accuse him unless we have some sort of evidence. If we do and he isn't guilty, we could do a great deal of harm."

Danny paced back and forth across the room.

"I tell you, Kay," he said, "we've got our hands full with this boy."

During the next few days, it seemed to Danny that Kent avoided him purposely. If Danny was sitting in the living room and Kent happened to come in, the boy would whirl on his heels and leave. If Danny came into a room where Kent was sitting, it was only a moment or two until Kent would get up and leave the room.

Danny mentioned it to Kay.

"I've never seen anyone act as guilty as he has the last few days," he told her. "I'm more convinced than ever that he didn't get that money honestly. It sticks out all over him."

"I hate to believe it, Danny, but I've got to agree with you," she replied. "All you have to do is to look at him and his face turns a fiery red."

"That's not all. I can't get close enough to him to talk to him. He's never been that way before."

Kay frowned. "But what do we do about it?"

"That's got me puzzled, too," Danny continued. "I don't like to accuse him of stealing the money unless we get some proof that he did. But if he has taken it from someone, the worst thing that could happen would be for him to get away with it."

Kay stood up. "We'll have to keep praying that God will guide and help us to make the right decision."

For a long while Danny sat in the living room, staring in silence at the wall.

* * *

The next afternoon when school was out, Kent came rushing into the Orlis home, his eyes sparkling with excitement. Jim was sprawled on the living room floor studying his history.

"Has anyone called for me, Jim?" he wanted to know.

Jim looked up at him.

"Nope. Not since I got home anyway. Is someone supposed to call you?"

Some of the life went out of Kent's eyes.

"I guess not." He crossed the room and sat down. "At least, I didn't know for sure whether I was going to get a call or not." He breathed deeply. "I- I just sort of thought maybe I would."

Jim went back to his studies. For a brief space of time Kent watched him.

"I'll bet you can't guess where I've been," Kent exclaimed at last.

Jim shrugged his shoulders.

"Jack Ross just took me for a ride in his car."

Jim snorted. "You don't call that an honor, do you? Most guys would be ashamed of it."

Kent laughed mirthlessly.

"The trouble with you is that you're jealous. That's all. We took his hot rod out to test it and do you know what we did?" He moved closer and lowered his voice. "We went ninety-seven miles an hour and he didn't even have 'er opened up!"

Jim closed his history book and reached for the English text at his elbow. "If you went ninety-seven miles an hour in a car with Jack Ross or anyone else, you're crazier than I thought you were."

Kent bristled. "Now, what do you mean by that?"

Jim sat in a chair.

"I think you know what I mean. It's against the law to drive that fast in the first place. And besides, you shouldn't associate with a guy who breaks the law."

"We didn't get caught," Kent answered, as though that was justification enough.

"Don't worry. If you keep that up, you will." Jim got up and moved to a chair closer to Kent. "Besides, did you ever stop to think what could happen to the car, and you, if a tie rod should break or you'd blow a tire while you were going at that speed?"

Kent grinned sheepishly.

"They'd be picking you up in a basket."

"You don't know how good a driver Jack is," Kent protested. "He can handle a car better than anyone else in this town. You should see the way he peels around corners."

Jim searched for the words he wanted to use. "I don't like to keep harping on this all the time," he said. "You probably think I sound like a broken record, but you shouldn't be running around with Jack Ross. I hate to see you ride to school with him, or even stop and talk to him on the street. The guy's bad medicine."

Kent straightened, and defiance gleamed in his eyes.

"You're just jealous, that's all. You're jealous because Jack won't take you with him. You're jealous because he's picked *me* as a friend, instead of you."

Jim shook his head vigorously. "That's not true, Kent," he said. "I don't care about riding with Jack or being his friend. Anybody who'll ride in that stupid car of his while he drives like a fool can be his friend if they want to. The only thing that bothers me about the whole deal is the way he can lead you into trouble." Jim's voice rose. "And I mean bad trouble. You might think for a while that you're having fun, but I'll guarantee you this much. If you run around with Jack Ross, you've had it."

Kent leaped to his feet, eyes blazing. "I've got to live here," he snorted, "but I don't have to sit and listen to you make fun of my friends!"

With that he stormed into the bedroom and slammed the door.

* * *

Danny got home early Saturday afternoon and was working around the house when Kent returned from town. The two of them were the only ones there.

"Hi, Kent," Danny said, as friendly as he could.

Kent only grunted under his breath.

"I'm glad you came back. I've been wanting to talk to you."

The boy's eyes blurred sullenly.

"Can't do it," he said lamely. "I–I've got to go back up town and–and see a guy."

Danny smiled disarmingly. "This won't take more than a few minutes. Besides, you look as hungry as I feel. Let's see if we can find something that'll make into a sandwich."

Kent Gilbert shook his head reluctantly.

"I–I don't care nothin' about gettin' somethin' to eat," he retorted. "I–I ain't hungry."

"Well, I'm hungry," Danny told him. "And I'll bet you'll want something to eat when you see one of my sandwiches."

In the kitchen over a cheese and peanut butter

sandwich and a glass of milk Danny began to talk to Kent about spiritual things.

"Have you ever thought anything about the Lord Jesus Christ and the claims He has on your life?" he asked quietly.

Kent shook his head.

"Nobody's got no claims on my life," he countered belligerently.

"Christ has a claim on your life, Kent," Danny said, "just as He has on mine."

"What do you mean?" he demanded, his lips curling expressively.

"The Bible says that each one of us is a sinner; that we have 'sinned and fall short of the glory of God.' In another place we are told that 'the wages of sin is death.' God doesn't want us to live as sinners. He doesn't want us to die and go into an eternity without Him. So He sent His Son, the Lord Jesus Christ, to die on earth for us."

Kent squirmed uncomfortably. "The preacher talked something about that the other Sunday, but I didn't pay much attention to it."

Danny leaned forward, his voice lowering.

"That's the trouble with a lot of people, Kent," he continued. 'They don't pay much attention to the fact that they've got to do something about Christ themselves. They ignore the fact that each person has to accept or reject Him. If they reject Him, they will be without excuse when they die and are sent to an eternity in hell."

Kent's face grew stony hard, but he said nothing in answer to Danny.

"Are you going to accept Christ as your Savior, Kent?" Danny asked.

Kent's expression did not change.

"I don't know."

"Or are you going to reject Him?"

Kent licked his lips nervously with the tip of his tongue.

"You can't ride the fence, you know," the youthful missionary went on. "You've got to get on one side or the other. It's Christ or Satan – heaven or hell. That's as certain for you as it is for me or any other person here on earth."

The boy was staring hard at the floor.

"If you don't decide for Christ," Danny went on, "you're deciding for Satan."

Kent looked up, eyes blazing angrily.

"Quit pushing me!" he snapped. "I know what I want to do."

"You think about what I've told you this afternoon, Kent," Danny said. "Think about it seriously. Kay and I will be praying for you."

Kent's mouth twisted in derision.

Danny waited.

"Is there something else you want to say, Kent?" he asked. "Do you have any questions?"

Kent shook his head. "Oh, skip it. You wouldn't like it if you knew what I think anyway." He turned and swaggered outside, slamming the door behind him.

# CHAPTER 7

# CAUGHT!

The following Monday afternoon Jim Morgan got a telephone call from the sporting goods store where he had ordered his new skis. After ending the call, he came back to the living room with his eyes shining.

"They're here, Danny!" he explained. "I can pick them up the first thing in the morning."

Danny grinned. "Now all we need is another five or six inches of snow," he said.

"Don't worry about that. There'll be plenty of snow sometime during the winter. There always is."

Danny put aside the newspaper. "Are you sure you've got money enough to pay for them?"

"You bet I have. I was just going in to count it." He went into his bedroom, but a moment later he came running back.

"Danny!" he cried. "It's gone!"

Danny stared at him queerly.

"What's gone?"

Jim's face was white and drawn. "The money I've been saving for my skis!" he said. "It's gone!"

Danny jumped to his feet.

"Are you sure about that, Jim?" he asked.

The boy's voice rose excitedly. "Sure, I'm sure of it. It wasn't more than a week ago that I counted it. It was all there then." His voice broke. "But it's gone now."

There was a short, painful silence.

"That's strange," Danny said. "That's very strange." He ran his hand through his hair. "Did anyone know where you kept it?"

Jim shook his head. "Not that I know of. I had it up in the closet on the shelf until Kent – until a few weeks ago." He faltered briefly. "Then I took it down and hid it in one of the dresser drawers – way down at the bottom, under all my clothes."

Danny thought for a moment.

"Would you recognize the money if you saw it again?" he asked. "Was there anything distinctive about any of the bills that would help you to recognize them now?"

"How could I see them again, Danny?" Jim demanded, anger rising. "Some character stole them."

"I've just got a hunch," Danny said. "That's all."

"I don't know for sure whether I could recognize any of the bills or not," Jim said slowly "There were two fives, a ten, and some ones. The rest of the money was in coins. Almost thirty dollars! And, I've been saving it just about forever!" He swallowed hard. "Now, I don't suppose I'll be able to get my new skis."

"Think hard, Jim," Danny persisted. "Do you remember anything special about those bills?"

Jim's forehead wrinkled.

"Well, now, let's see," he said. "One of the five-dollar bills had a corner torn off it. At least I seem to remember it that way. And the other was all curled and crinkly, as though somebody had left it rolled up for a long time. I unrolled it, but it wouldn't stay flat."

"I imagine a lot of five-dollar bills over the country could be described that way," Danny murmured, more to himself than to Jim. He went into the other room and a moment or two later came back. "Does this look like one of your bills?"

Jim took it in his hand and turned it slowly.

"That's one of them," he announced.

"Are you sure?"

"I'm positive," Jim assured him. "Look at the way that corner's torn off. It looks like someone took a bite out of it." He breathed deeply. "This is one of the bills, all right. Where did you get it, Danny?"

Danny's eyes darkened.

"I think you've got a pretty good idea," he said.

"Kent?"

"That's right. I'm going to have another talk with him when he gets home."

* * *

Almost two hours passed before Kent came back into the house. He scowled belligerently when he saw Jim and Danny sitting there and would have passed without speaking, but Danny stopped him.

"Hello, Kent."

"Hi."

He went through the living room and opened his bedroom door.

"Just a minute, Kent," Danny said. "I'd like to talk to you."

"Ain't got time." The color crept into Kent's cheeks. "I–I just came home to get something."

He went into the bedroom and closed the door. Danny got to his feet decisively.

"Kent," he said, "come out here. We want to talk to you."

There was a long silence. Then Kent opened the door and came out to face them.

"Well," he demanded, "what'm I supposed to've done this time?"

"We want to ask you some questions," Danny said coldly. "Sit down."

"I'd rather stand."

"I said for you to sit down!" Danny ordered in a stern voice. "That's just what I mean!"

Kent stomped over to a chair and plopped down.

"Now, I hope you're satisfied."

Danny completely ignored his remark.

"Kent," he said evenly, "I'd like to know where you got the money."

"What money?"

His face had drained white, and for a brief instant his gaze lowered.

"You know what money I'm talking about as well as I do."

"L-like I told you, Danny, I–I got this job helping a guy. He was real satisfied with the way I worked, so he gave me a good tip. That's all there is to it."

Danny shook his head.

"I can't buy that, Kent. Who is this guy? And what sort of work did you do for him?"

"What good would it do for me to tell you? You wouldn't believe me."

Danny moved a step closer to Kent and stared down at him.

"As a matter of fact, you didn't work for anyone, Kent," he said coldly. "You took that money from Jim's room. You deliberately stole it!"

"I did not!" Kent's indignation sounded genuine.

"Don't lie to me!" Danny retorted. "That'll only make matters worse."

"I'm not lying to you. I didn't steal that money from Jim." Kent's face darkened. "But it wouldn't do any good for me to tell you what happened. You wouldn't believe me, anyway."

"When you tell me the truth, I'll be glad to believe

you. I knew you couldn't have earned that money as quickly as you said you did, but I couldn't say anything about it because I didn't have any evidence." He paused, eyes searching the boy's thin face. "I've got the evidence now. Jim's ski money is gone!"

Kent snorted angrily.

"And I suppose he's trying to blame it on me," he said. "That's the way it is around here. If anything happens, you all start screaming at me. I'm getting sick of it!"

"As a matter of fact," Danny said, "Jim didn't even mention you until I did. But as soon as he told me he'd been robbed, I knew where you'd gotten that money. I showed him one of the bills, and he identified it."

"How could a guy identify a bill?" Kent blustered. "There are millions of 'em. You're just tryin' to hang this on me, that's all."

"I'm going to ask you for the last time where you got that money, Kent," Danny continued. "If you earned it, I want to know whom you worked for so we can go to see him and check out your story. If you stole it from Jim, I want to know that, too."

Kent straightened. "For your information I didn't steal that money from anyone. And what's more, you can't prove it!"

Danny's gaze met his.

"Is that your answer?"

"That's right! And you'd just as well quit givin' me the third degree! You're not goin' to get me to say anything different!"

Danny turned on his heel and went and picked up his phone. Fear leaped into Kent's eyes.

"What're you goin' to do, Danny?"

Danny did not stop dialing. "I'm going to use my phone."

"Who're you calling?"

Kent got up and came over to where Danny was standing.

"I told you I was going to give you one last chance to tell me where you got the money," Danny said. "But you decided to lie to me, so I'm calling the sheriff. He knows how to handle matters like this."

Eyes widening, Kent stared as Danny started to tap the numbers on his phone. Danny just started to tap the fifth digit when Kent's hand darted out and stopped him.

"Don't call him, Danny!" he cried. "I–I took the money!" With that he started to sob uncontrollably.

Danny put the phone down and turned to face Kent.

"Let's go back and sit down," he said. "I want to get the entire story from the very beginning."

"Wh-wh-what are you going to do to me?" Kent blurted out. "Are you going to have me put in jail? Are you, Danny?"

Danny paused.

"I want to know exactly what happened, Kent," he repeated, "and why you took the money. There'll be plenty of time for us to talk about your punishment after we find out just what took place."

Kent's lips were trembling so much he could scarcely speak.

"Jim always was braggin' about them new skis he was gettin' and how much fun he was goin' to have with 'em," he began, stumbling over the words. "I–I've never had nothin' nice myself, and I–I–" He looked pleadingly at Danny. "And I felt so bad when I got my clothes ruined and you said you were goin' to make me pay for 'em that I–I guess I just–" His voice trailed off to nothing.

"Kent, you're tryin' to blame Jim and me for what you did."

"Well–."

"In the first place, Jim hasn't been bragging about those new skis," Danny countered. "He's worked hard for them, and he's saved the money after paying his tithe and buying all his own clothes. He has every right to own a new pair of skis, and you had no right to keep him from getting them by stealing his money."

Kent swallowed hard.

"I wouldn't have done it if you hadn't made me pay for those clothes," he flared. "It was your fault."

"Now wait a minute," Danny broke in. "I told you that you had to get a job and give me half the money you earned until you paid for your clothes. A lot of times Jim hasn't had half of his paper route money left for himself."

"I–I–" The boy's lips waggled helplessly, but the words would not come out.

"The truth of the matter is," Danny continued, "that you were jealous of Jim and desperate to get money so you could show me you didn't have to go to work. That's why you stole Jim's paper route money, isn't it?"

There was no answer. Kent continued to sob fearfully.

After a time, he looked up.

"Wh-wh-what are you goin' to do to me, Danny?" Desperation edged his voice.

"That's something I haven't decided yet."

"You–you ain't goin' to put me in jail, are you, Danny? Are you?"

Danny took a long time in answering.

"Kent," he said finally, "you've been belligerent and antagonistic to Kay and me ever since you came to live with us. You've resisted every effort we've made to try to help you. And you haven't been satisfied even with that. You've done everything you could to show us you don't like us, and you've tried to get Jill to go along with you in your warped thinking against us."

Danny took a deep breath.

"In the light of all those things, can you give me one good reason why we shouldn't turn this matter over to the authorities and let them handle it?"

Kent started to cry once more. His frail shoulders shook.

# CHAPTER 8

# A JOB FOR KENT

Panic leaped to Kent Gilbert's eyes and stole the color from his thin cheeks. For an agonizing instant he stared at Danny. He put his trembling hand on the young missionary pilot's arm. His fingers tightened convulsively and, when he spoke, his voice was taut and faltering.

"Wh-wh-what are you goin' to do to me, Danny?" He could scarcely force out the words. "What're you goin' to do to me?"

"I haven't decided yet."

"Kent's voice raised. "You–you ain't goin' to turn me over to the police, are you?"

Danny's lips narrowed.

"I don't know why I shouldn't," he said. "You've broken the law, Kent. You knew it was wrong, but you deliberately stole from Jim. Can you give me a good reason why I shouldn't call the authorities?"

"I–I'll never do it again, Danny! You can depend on that. I promise. I–I'll never take anything from anyone else as long as I live. I've learned my lesson!" He sucked in his breath sharply. "Only don't call the p-police. They'll send me to the reformatory. Don't call 'em, Danny. Please!"

There was a brief silence.

"You say that you'll never do it again, Kent," Danny said sternly, "and you sound as though you mean it."

"I do!" Kent had stopped crying. "Believe me, Danny! I mean it!"

"But you sounded as though you were telling me the truth when you said you didn't take the money," Danny continued. "How do I know when to believe you?"

Kent's lower lip trembled.

"If–if Jim Morgan was in my place," he stammered, "I–I'll bet you wouldn't call the cops to–to take him away. You've got it in for me, that's all. You're trying to get rid of me!"

A big tear slipped from beneath his eyelid and rolled down his cheek.

"If you hadn't been pickin' on me, I wouldn't have done it. You kept houndin' me about payin' back the money I owed you. That's why I did it! I had to get you off my back!"

Anger flared in Danny's voice.

"Kent Gilbert," he snapped, "that's not true, and you know it! If we wanted to get rid of you, all we would have to do is call Mr. Collins at the welfare office and tell him to come and get you. It'd be a lot easier than all of this."

"I–I–" Kent swallowed hard.

Danny took a deep breath. "I–I'm sorry I lost my temper, Kent, but it did disturb me when you made a claim like that. You can't blame me or anyone else for the fix you're in. You're the one who stole that money – the only one. And you're going to have to pay the consequences."

The boy stifled a sob. "Danny," he said brokenly, "if you'll let me off just this one time, you won't be sorry. I'll never do anything like that again. I promise."

Danny's voice grew even more serious.

"I suppose there are those who would say that this stealing episode is the worst sin in your life, Kent," he said in measured tones. "But it isn't."

Kent looked up defensively.

"What're you tryin' to blame me for now?" he demanded. "Ain't I in enough trouble already?"

"I'm not blaming you for anything. I'm just say-ing that stealing isn't your biggest sin. The biggest sin in your life is that you have rejected Christ as your Savior."

Kent shot Danny a questioning glance. "I don't get what you're talkin' about. What's that got to do with takin' Jim's money?"

"Everything. You've tried to rule your life yourself. You've refused to become a Christian and let God take over, so Satan has had full sway in your life. You see, we're ruled either by God or by Satan. The choice is ours. But we're all under the control of one or the other."

Once more Kent's lips started to quiver.

I'll never do anything like this again, Danny," he protested desperately. "And I–I'll just do anything for you if you promise not to turn me over to the police. I–I'll get a job and pay the money back, and I–I'll go to church without complaining, and I'll study hard on my homework and–."

Danny thought for a moment.

"How much money do you have left, Kent?" he asked.

The boy took off his shoe and removed several bills from it.

"I–I don't have very much. I gave you eleven dollars and I–" He acted as though he was going to tell what he had done with the rest of the money, but he did not. "Here's six dollars, and I've got some change in my dresser drawer. I–I'll get that, too. And I'll get a job right away and give every cent of the money to Jim until I pay back all I owe him." His voice choked until he could not speak.

"It won't be easy to work and pay back Jim," Danny said slowly. "I'll give him the money you gave me, but you will still owe me. And you'll have to pay him the rest of what you owe him. It's not going to be easy."

"But if you'll give me half a chance, Danny, I'll pay it back. I'll pay back every single cent of it. Only–only don't let them send me to jail," Kent cried.

Danny crossed the room and came back again to stand before him.

"I know of a job you could get, Kent," he replied. "The pay isn't too good, though, and the work would be hard."

"That won't make any difference," Kent assured him. "I don't care what the job is or how hard it is. I can do it. I know I can! I'll work all the time. I'll even quit school and go to work if you want me to."

Danny shook his head.

"You have to stay in school," he said. "Dropping out wouldn't solve anything."

"Then I'll stay in school and study harder than I've ever studied in my life," Kent continued.

"This job I've been thinking about is working for an elderly couple on the other side of town. They need someone to carry in coal, to carry out the ashes, and to shovel the walks when it snows. Then there'll be some odd jobs around the place. It isn't easy work, but it is a job you could handle. And you should be able to earn enough money between now and the time school is out to pay Jim back what you owe him."

Kent brightened. "Then you're goin' to let me off this time, Danny?"

"Not exactly," Danny said. "I'm going to talk this over with the authorities. I feel they have a right to know what's happened. Then we're going to have to put some sort of limitation on your activities. You're going to have to be home at nights except for activities at church and a limited number of school activities.

You'll have to keep up your homework and not play hooky or anything of that sort. In short, Kent, you're going to have to prove to us that you're worthy of being trusted again."

Kent sighed his relief.

"Oh, thank you, Danny!" he exclaimed. "You don't know how this makes me feel. I–I–"

Danny's expression was still stern and unbending. "If you prove yourself in these things, Kent," he said, "you'll have done all we expect of you. But I won't do the same thing a second time. If I find you have broken the law again, I'll have no other course except to turn you over to the proper authorities."

Kent replied quickly.

"You won't have to worry about me, Danny. I–I've learned my lesson."

"I hope so," Danny said. "I sincerely hope so."

* * *

During the next few days Kent Gilbert seemed to be a changed boy. Every night when he came home from school he went directly to his room and concentrated on his homework until he finished it. And when the evening meal was over, he helped with the dishes. He even kept his room clean and made his bed each morning without being reminded.

He worked for Mr. and Mrs. Watkins on Saturdays and at least one afternoon a week.

After Kent had worked several times, Danny checked with Mr. Watkins to see if he was working satisfactorily.

"Oh, we're so happy with Kent," Mr. Watkins said. "I don't think we've ever had a boy work for us who has worked as hard or has done as well as he has. I can't thank you enough for helping us get him, Danny."

"I'm glad to hear he's working out so well," Danny replied.

That evening when the younger members of the family were all in bed, Danny told Kay what Mr. Watkins had said. She was as pleased as he had been.

"You know, Danny," she said, "maybe something like this is all Kent needed to see that we're behind him."

Danny took a deep breath.

"I'll have to admit that it does surprise me a little to see him taking hold the way he has been. I didn't figure he would be the sort of a kid who would respond so quickly."

Kay smiled.

"We've been praying for him, Danny. We can expect things to happen."

Danny was silent for a moment.

"Yes," he said at last, "we can expect things to happen. But we don't want to forget that he hasn't made a decision for Christ yet. All that any of this actually means is that Kent is trying to reform himself. And you know what shaky ground that is."

Kay's eyes darkened. "I'd never thought of it that way."

# CHAPTER 9

# A CHRISTMAS SURPRISE

Linda Penner met Jack Ross in the hall at school one afternoon shortly before Christmas vacation. He stopped her at her locker as she was getting her coat.

"Hi, kitten," he said, grinning. "And just where've you been keeping yourself all these weeks? I thought maybe you'd gone off and gotten married or something."

She smiled at him. "Don't tell me you've missed me."

"How could I help it?" His smile faded. "It's been a long time, kitten."

"I've been busy." She picked up her books to leave, but Jack blocked her path.

"You wouldn't be so busy if you didn't run to everything that goes on at that church of yours. If you were like you used to be, you'd have a little time for good old Jack Ross."

Linda blushed.

"Please, Jack," she said. "Don't talk that way. You know what being a Christian means to me. You know that things will never be the way they used to be."

"Maybe not, but I can't help feeling you're missing a lot." He lowered his voice. "I'm really in the dough now. If you'd just let me, I could show you a good time you'd never forget."

She took half a step forward, but he put out a hand and stopped her once more.

"Don't rush off," he said. "I've got something to show you."

He fished a roll of bills from his pocket and flashed it before her eyes.

In spite of herself, Linda gasped. "Jack! Where'd you get all that money?"

"What's the matter?" Jack asked teasingly. "Are you surprised to see that I've got a little cash?"

For a moment she stared at him.

"A little!" she echoed. "Why, there must be over a hundred dollars there."

"And there's more where that came from."

The surprise left Linda's face. "Where did you get it, Jack?"

He laughed mysteriously. "Didn't I tell you? I'm in business now."

"Business?"

"Sure, I've even got some guys working for me." He walked beside her to the door. "You know, Linda, you can't make any real money working for some-body else. If a guy wants to get in the dough, he's got to get something working for himself." At the outside door he stopped and turned to face her. "If you were still going with me, you could have any-thing you wanted."

"No, thank you."

"We'd really do the town."

"No, thank you," she repeated. "That's all over and done with."

Disappointment filled his eyes.

"Well," he said, trying hard to act as though it really didn't matter much, "the least you could do is ride home with me. You haven't had a ride in a real car for a couple of months."

Linda hesitated. "No, thanks. I think I'd better walk."

"It's awfully cold outside, and you've got almost a mile to go. Better change your mind."

She said nothing.

"Now, Linda," he continued, "don't be that way. You're the only girl I ever have thought anything of. Give me a break just once, won't you?"

"Well–" Her voice caught slightly. "Well, I'll ride with you if you'll take me straight home. I can't ride around."

"Sure! Sure! Anything you say! I knew you weren't as gone on that religion as you pretended to be. I'll bet you've been getting tired of sitting around home waiting for something to happen."

They left the schoolhouse together. Linda felt a flush of excitement at being with Jack again. Just getting into his car brought flames to her cheeks and quickened the rhythm of her heart. At the same time, her very being ached. Was she really doing what she should? Should she even accept a ride home with Jack Ross?

The powerful engine started with a deep-throated roar, and she leaned back in the seat and closed her eyes. There was no denying it. It was fun to be with Jack again. It was a lot of fun.

* * *

At the Orlis home Danny and Kay were busy getting ready for Christmas.

"You know, Kay, it was a wonderful idea to ask Ron, Darlene, and Dad and Mother to come and spend Christmas with us."

She came over and sat on the arm of his chair.

"It is going to seem a little strange not going back to the Angle for Christmas," she said, "but I thought it would be nice to have them come here. It won't make so much work for Mother Orlis."

"And it'll be easier for them to come here than it would be for all of us to go up there," Danny reminded her.

Kent came into the room just then. Danny turned and greeted him.

"Hi, Kent. Are you already through working at the Watkins'?"

The boy scowled and a sullen fire glittered in his dark eyes.

"I wouldn't have come home if I hadn't been," he retorted, going over and sitting in a chair near the window. "What's goin' on around here, anyway?"

"We're having company tomorrow," Kay explained. "Danny's mother and father are coming to spend Christmas with us. So I'm trying to get all the work done before they get here."

The boy snorted derisively.

"I don't know why people get so shook up about Christmas," he said. "It don't mean nothin' to me."

"It should," Danny told him. "It's the day we observe the birth of the Lord Jesus Christ. Christmas and Easter are the biggest days of the year to me."

Kent shrugged his shoulders.

"That's swell. That's just great," he went on. "Only don't expect me to do no handstands about it."

"What was Christmas like at your home, Kent?" Danny asked. "How did you and your parents observe it when you were living with them?"

Bitterness twisted his young face.

"Well, there wasn't no presents, for one thing. Me an' Jill ain't never had no Christmas presents that I can remember. It just meant another bottle of booze to our old man, and the chance that we'd get a good beatin' before he sobered up."

The hurt showed in Kay's eyes.

* * *

The next afternoon Carl and Mary Orlis came down to Fairview by bus. After dinner and devotions that evening, they all sat around talking endlessly. Danny and Kay asked about the neighbors on the Angle. And Mr. and Mrs. Orlis wanted to know about Danny's work and the activities of their church. After a time, Kent, Jill, and Jim went off to bed. As soon as they were out of the room, Kay turned to Mary Orlis.

"Well," she said, "what do you think of Kent and Jill?"

"They're certainly needy children," the older woman observed. "There's a strange, haunted look about them. They must have been miserable at home."

"I'm sure they were."

"Somehow Kent reminds me of Jim before he was saved. He's got that same look about him – the same belligerence and secrecy."

Danny nodded. "He reminds me of Jim, too. And we've had some of the same sort of trouble with him that you had with Jim before he accepted Christ as his Savior."

"We're hoping he's learned his lesson, though." Kay related the incident of the stolen money. "He's certainly a lot better now, or at least he seems to be. In fact, we've had difficulty in realizing he's the same boy."

Carl Orlis, who had not said much before, straightened in his chair.

"I'm always glad when anyone who's been in difficulty seems to be better than they were," he said, "but we don't want to lose sight of the fact that we cannot improve ourselves without the help of the Lord. And we can't have the Lord's help unless we have confessed our sin and accepted Jesus Christ as our personal Savior." He took a deep breath. "You didn't say anything about Kent making a decision for Christ, so I suppose this reforming is all on his own?"

"That's what I told Kay the other night," Danny put in. "We can be glad for any little improvement in his conduct, but there's nothing solid to build on until he gets right with God."

Mother Orlis' face was serious.

"We'll have to be in prayer a lot for him and his sister," she said. "They need the Lord so very, very much."

* * *

Two days before Christmas, Ron Orlis and Darlene Snyder drove in from Cedarton Bible Institute. They came into the house, stamping the snow from their feet, their cheeks stung red by the bitter cold. Danny started for the door.

"I'll go out and get your bags."

Jim followed him. "I'll help you."

Once they were outside Jim turned to Danny and asked, "Why'd Ron have to drag *her* along?"

"I think maybe he likes to have her with him. She's a lovely Christian girl."

"Yeah." Jim's disgust showed through. "But I had some plans for Ron while he was home. We were goin' skiing and a lot of things."

"You can still do that," Danny told him. "I'll bet Darlene enjoys skiing."

Jim snorted. "Take her along?" he exclaimed. "You know what that'd be like, don't you? He'd be talking to her all the time and helping her ski and wondering if she'd like to have something warm to drink, or asking her if she didn't think the view was beautiful. No, thank you. I couldn't stand it!"

Danny laughed.

"Now, what's the matter with you?" Jim demanded irritably.

"You sound like Ron did a few years ago when I brought Kay home for the first time," Danny told him. "And now look at him." He put an arm about the boy's shoulders. "Just wait. You'll be doing the same thing in a few years."

Jim shook his head vigorously. "Not me. I know better."

"One of these days a pretty little gal will turn her big brown eyes on you and smile," Danny continued in a teasing manner, "and you'll be a goner, just like all the rest of us."

Jim jerked a suitcase out of the trunk.

"You just wait. You'll see!"

That evening in the living room Darlene turned to Ron. "Do you think we should tell them?"

"Tell us what?" Kay wanted to know.

Ron flushed. "Why don't you do it?"

"I think it would be better if you did. They're your parents."

Ron swallowed hard.

"Well," he stammered, "I–I mean–"

Danny broke in quickly.

"Go ahead, Ron," he said. "I don't think you're revealing a secret to us. When's it going to be?"

"We–we've been talking it over, and we've decided to–to get married as soon as school's out."

Kay went over impulsively and threw her arms about Darlene.

"Oh, Darlene!" she exclaimed. "That's wonderful!"

Horror stood in Jim's eye. *Oh, no! Not that!*

# CHAPTER 10

# KENT'S NIGHT OUT

Ron Orlis and Darlene Snyder left Fairview the day after Christmas for Darlene's home in the Twin Cities area. Everyone went out to the porch when they were ready to leave. Jim pushed up beside Ron.

"Boy," he said, "I wish you didn't have to leave so soon. We didn't get to do anything I'd planned."

"It was a short stay, Jim," Ron answered. "Maybe we can do a little better the next time."

Jim's face darkened. "What do you mean, 'we'? Are you going to be bringing Darlene along *every* time you come?"

"Every chance I get."

Jim shook his head.

"I'll never figure you out, Ron," he said. "You used to be *one* guy I could always count on to go skiing or ice fishing or rabbit hunting. I never thought some girl would get her hooks into you and make a different guy out of you."

Danny came over to them just then.

"Say, Ron, would you like to have me go along and talk to Darlene's dad for you?"

Jim turned to him quickly.

"Why would Ron want you to go along and talk to Mr. Snyder, Danny? What's this all about?"

"I thought maybe Ron would want me to go along and put in a good word for him when he asks for her hand," Danny answered. "I could tell Mr. Snyder what a fine, upstanding young man Ron is and how glad we are that he's finally found some girl who'll put up with him."

"You'd be a big help," Ron said, laughing. "I can see that. I believe I'd better do my own asking."

Then they were gone. Danny and Kay and the others went back into the house.

"It was certainly good to have Ron and Darlene with us, wasn't it?" Danny asked.

"I'm so happy for them," Kay said.

"As far as I'm concerned," Jim put in, frowning, "Ron could just as well have stayed in Cedarton. Do you know I didn't even get to spend *one* afternoon with him without *her* tagging along."

"Watch what you say, Jim," Danny warned. "You'll be in the same boat yourself in a few years."

"No sir, not me." He shook his head firmly. "You'll never see the day when I get so wrapped up in a girl that I won't go skiing alone with a guy who–who's practically my brother."

Kay sat down across from him in the living room.

"I'd like to have a tape recording of that, Jim. It's something I would enjoy playing back to you some day."

He snorted disdainfully. "You just wait. You'll see.

* * *

The following morning after Danny had left for a flying trip that would take him away for several days, Kay had an errand for Kent to run.

"I'm going to need some soap right away so that I can finish washing," she told him. "Please hurry."

"You don't have to give me a bad time," he grumbled. "I'll get your old soap and get it back here as soon as I can. Seems like I can't do anything around here anymore without getting a nice little lecture along with it."

Kay did not lose her temper.

"I didn't mean to give you a lecture, Kent," she said. "I just wanted you to know that I can't finish washing without the soap, so please come right back from the store."

He got into his parka and heavy overshoes.

"OK, OK. I'll get your old soap for you." he was still growling to himself when he went out into the cold morning air.

When he turned the corner and headed toward town, Jack Ross was sitting at the curb waiting for him.

"I thought you were never going to come along," he said. "I've been waiting out here for half an hour."

"I told you I didn't know if I'd be able to get out this morning."

"Kay and Danny sure keep a close watch on you, Kent," Jack spouted.

A scowl twisted Kent's face.

"You can say that again. And I'm gettin' awful tired of it."

Jack meshed the gears smoothly.

"I've got to go to the supermarket and get a box of soap," Kent went on. "And if I don't get right back, Kay's goin' to skin me alive."

"OK. OK. I'll get you to the store. But I want to talk to you first. You shouldn't let Kay and Danny bother you so much. You don't have to let them get away with orderin' you around."

"You can talk," Kent protested. "You don't know what it's like. They seem to spend all their time just watchin' me. They know everything I do."

Jack shrugged. "All you've got to do is do like I say, and you can fool 'em easy."

Kent turned in the seat. "You can do a lot of talkin'," he said. "You ain't the one who has to put up with em.

"Maybe not," Jack continued, "but I know how to fool 'em. All you've got to do is listen to me, and you've got it made."

He turned the corner and pulled up before the town's largest supermarket.

"And you can start tonight."

Kent's eyes narrowed fearfully.

"Tonight?"

"Yeah. Tonight. That's what I wanted to see you about. I'm gettin' some of the guys together after supper. We've got a little work to do." He winked significantly.

Kent swallowed hard.

"Wh-wh-what kind of work?"

Jack lowered his voice.

"You be there tonight, and I'll tell you all about it."

Kent spoke in a hoarse whisper. "I–I don't know whether I can even get out tonight. Kay watches me like a hawk all the time."

Jack's lips curled.

"You be there, buddy! That's all I've got to say!"

The rest of the day dragged on endlessly for Kent. Kay had some work for him to do when he got home with the soap, and he didn't get at his studying until after lunch. He planned on studying all afternoon, but after a few minutes he made an excuse to go downtown once more. He was glad he didn't see Jack Ross again.

At dinner that evening Kent fidgeted uneasily. Kay noticed it and turned to him.

"Kent," she said, "is something wrong?"

He looked up quickly.

"Wrong?" he echoed. "Why would there be anything wrong?"

"I don't know, but you've acted so strangely this afternoon, and now you're scarcely eating a bite."

"I ain't hungry," Kent replied.

"Are you sure you feel all right?" Kay asked.

His temper flared. "I just don't feel like eating, that's all. There ain't no law against that, is there?"

Kay started to answer sternly, but she stopped. Kent took a small helping of food and sat there toying with it the rest of the meal. When they had finished eating, Kay got out the Bible, and they had their devotions. Kent said nothing while she was reading, but there was a detached look in his eyes. It seemed as though he was listening without actually hearing anything that was read.

As soon as their devotions were finished, he pushed back from the table.

"You know, Kay," he said, "I forgot to get some notebook paper when I was downtown this afternoon." He got to his feet. "I'm going to have to get some before I can finish my homework." He started for the closet where he kept his coat. "I'll be back after a while."

Kay got up quickly.

"Oh, I think I have some paper here. Jim bought a ream a week or so ago."

"I wouldn't think of taking anything that belonged to Jim. I'll just go down and get some. I won't be gone long."

Kay did not yield.

"No, we have plenty of paper here," she said. "You can get some the next time you're in town and pay Jim back. He won't mind."

"But–."

She did not listen to his protest, but went into the other room and came back a moment later with the paper.

He took it grumpily.

"I'd just as well go down and get some of my own. I've got to have a new ballpoint pen before I can get to work. I–I broke mine yesterday."

"I've got a ball point you can have," Kay answered. "I was given one in a store while I was shopping yesterday."

Kent took the pen, grunted something or other to her, and went to his room. At his desk he pulled out the chair and sat down. He had to get out. He just had to! Jack and the guys would blow a fuse if he kicked out on them now. But how was he going to accomplish it? That was the question.

A few minutes later he went into the other room and tried again.

"Kay," he said, "is it all right if I go down to the library for a little while? There are some reference books I've just got to have."

She came into the room where he was standing.

"I thought you told me you didn't have any home-work over the weekend," she said.

His eyes did not waver as his gaze met hers.

"You must've misunderstood me, Kay," he told her. "We *always* have homework to do. It don't make any difference when it is, they pile on the work. I think the teachers here just try to see how hard they can make it. And they won't give any extra time, either." He paused to see if his words were having any effect on her. "So, if I don't get to the library, I won't be able to get my lesson on time. I'll flunk, that's what'll happen."

Kay hesitated momentarily.

"The library will be open tomorrow afternoon, Kent," she said. "I'd much rather have you go then."

His eyes narrowed.

"But I can't go tomorrow afternoon," he protested in desperation. "If I can't go to the library now, I won't be able to get my work in on time."

There was a firmness in Kay's voice that was seldom present when she talked with Kent.

"If you can't go to the library tomorrow," she informed him, "you'll just have to miss out on this assignment. You're not to go tonight."

His eyes blazed in fury.

"All right! If you want me to flunk, it's all right with me! You're the one who's been after me to study and get good grades. Now you won't let me go to the library so I can."

Kay made no comment.

Kent glared at her, bewilderment and anger mixing in his face.

He turned on his heel, stormed into his bedroom, and slammed the door. Now he was really in a spot! He had to get out to be with Jack and the guys. That was all there was to it. They were counting on him.

But how?

He walked to the window and looked out across the snow-covered yard. Slowly an idea came. It might work. It just might work – if only Kay and Jill went to bed early enough.

Then he went into the other room, picked up the paper, and sat down. After a few minutes he got to his feet.

"I'm sleepy tonight," he said. "I think I'll go to bed."

"That sounds like a good idea," Kay said. "As soon as I finish ironing, I think I'll go to bed too. I haven't been able to catch up on my sleep since Danny's parents were here."

Jill looked up, disappointment in her eyes.

"I'm not sleepy," she said. "I'm not a bit sleepy. I don't see why I have to go to bed so early."

Kay's smile was warm and understanding.

"You know, when I was a girl about your age, my mother used to let me go to bed and read once in a while. I thought it was great fun."

Jill brightened.

Kent wanted to protest, but he dared not. That would give everything away.

It probably wouldn't hurt to have Jill awake for a little while, he reasoned. She wouldn't hear anything. And if she did, he could keep her quiet easily. He went into his bedroom, slipped off his shoes, and crawled into bed. Tensely he lay there until long after he heard Kay go into her bedroom and turn off the lights. Then he got up, slipped on his shoes quietly, opened the window, and slipped out.

For an instant or two his heart beat fiercely against his ribs. Kay must have heard him! He was sure of it!

But there was no sound.

Hurriedly he closed the window and rushed to the place where Jack and the guys were to meet.

As he suspected, Jack was furious.

"Well, it's about time you got here."

"I came as fast as I could."

"We don't want any more of your excuses," Jack blustered. "When I tell you to be here, I mean you're to be here. Understand?"

Kent swallowed hard and nodded. A vague uneasiness crept over him. But he could not back out now – even though he wanted to. He couldn't have all the guys laughing at him.

# CHAPTER 11

# TRACKS IN THE SNOW

Apprehensively, very late that night, Kent Gilbert came back to the Orlis home and slipped as quietly as possible through the window into his room. His heart was hammering fiercely against his rib cage, and perspiration gleamed on his young forehead.

For the space of a heartbeat or two he stood before the half-open window, panting for breath. It had all seemed so important earlier in the evening that he not let Jack and the guys down. Now he fervently wished that he had.

He would never get away with this. He couldn't. Kay probably had heard him leave, or had gotten up and checked his room while he was gone. If she hadn't, she surely would have heard him open the window and slip in. He'd made a little noise climbing over the sill – enough to have awakened her. She was probably at the telephone calling the police right now.

Numbly Kent skinned out of his clothes and crawled into bed. He stared up into the darkness. After Danny had caught him stealing from Jim, he had made up his mind he was never going to get into a mess like that again.

But he had.

And even now the cops might be on their way to get him. His mouth worked nervously, and he began to tremble.

A car went by outside. He raised up on one elbow and peered out. Perhaps that was the cops now. Perhaps they wouldn't even wait until morning but would come charging up to the house and jerk him out of bed. Scalding tears welled in his eyes and coursed down his cheeks.

Jack Ross was never going to get him into a deal like this again. That was one thing for sure! If he ever got out of this without going to the reformatory, he would never let *anyone* talk him into breaking the law again.

Kent turned over on his side and closed his eyes. In spite of that, all he could see was uniformed officers in their police car. And they were after him! *They were after him!*

And when they caught him, he'd be all alone, he knew. Danny Orlis wouldn't stick up for him, and neither would anyone else. The cops would send him off to the reform school or do whatever they wanted to do with him! An anguished sob shook his frail shoulders.

The following morning Kent was up an hour before his usual time. He was sitting in the living room trying to read a magazine and forget what he had done the night before, when his sister, Jill, came tiptoeing in. Her eyes were round with fright and accusation.

"What's the matter with you?" Kent demanded.

Jill's voice was a hoarse whisper. "You were supposed to be home last night," she said. "You weren't supposed to go anywhere – but you did!"

Kent sat bolt upright, his face going ashen.

"Who says I wasn't home last night?" he asked.

She looked about to make sure she wasn't overheard. "I went to the window a little while ago to see if it had snowed again during the night, and do you know what I saw?"

He moistened his lips with the tip of his tongue.

"I saw your tracks outside your window." Her voice was taut. "You sneaked out last night after we went to bed."

Kent ran a hand nervously over his chalk-white face.

"I did not," he blustered defensively. "I was right in bed all the time. You're just imagining things."

Jill stood her ground.

"You come with me, Kent," she persisted, "and I'll show you the tracks. They're just as plain as can be. Anybody can tell what you did."

The corners of Kent's mouth twitched nervously.

"I–I didn't go out through the window, Jill," he protested lamely. "I–I just happened to be outside a little while before supper and went up to the window. That–that's how I happened to make the tracks you saw."

She was still unconvinced.

"I don't know what you were doing last night, Kent," she went on, her voice taut, "but I know you weren't in your room all the time. You can't fool me!"

He leaned over quickly and grasped both her shoulders.

"Don't you tell anybody that!" he exclaimed. "If you do, you'll get me into a lot of trouble–trouble I won't be able to get out of! Do you understand?"

Fear widened her eyes.

"I–I won't tell anybody you sneaked out last night, Kent," she whispered. "Honest, I won't. I won't even tell Kay."

"You'd better not tell anybody! Especially Kay! You'd just better not tell anything, if you know what's good for you!"

He did not relax his grip on her thin shoulders.

"Kent, don't!" she cried out. "You're hurting me!"

At that moment Kay came to the kitchen door and called them to breakfast. Kent's eyes searched his young sister's face questioningly.

"You won't tell on me, will you?" he asked.

"I–I already told you I won't."

At the breakfast table Kay eyed Kent curiously. "Did you sleep well last night?" she asked him.

"I–I guess so." He stumbled over the words.

"I was surprised you went to bed so early. Jill and I popped some corn and thought you might want some."

He shrugged his shoulders with exaggerated indifference.

"I was too sleepy to eat any popcorn last night."

When they had finished eating, Kent got his parka and overshoes and left the house. Jack Ross was waiting for him in his car two or three blocks up the street. Jack glanced at his watch.

"Late again!" he said disgustedly.

"I came just as soon as I could, Jack," Kent answered. "Honest I did. You don't know what it's like to get away from Kay Orlis. She's suspicious of everything I do."

Jack slammed his car into gear and went careening up the street. "Do you think I've nothing else to do except to wait on you?" he asked irritably. "Well, for your information, I'm getting tired of having you show up late all the time."

There was a brief silence.

"I–I don't believe I'm going to be able to–to work for you anymore, Jack," Kent stuttered.

Jack laughed.

"I felt the same way the first time I took anything, but after a while you get so it doesn't bother you anymore." He fished his billfold from his pocket. "Especially when you come to the payoff."

Kent watched him silently.

"Here's five bucks," Jack said, waving a bill before his eyes. "This is your share of last night's take. Not bad, is it?"

"Five dollars?" Kent could scarcely believe it.

"That's just about the easiest money you ever earned," Jack said. "How long did it take us? About an hour. You can't beat that."

"Have you s-s-sold the stuff already?"

Once more Jack laughed.

"I had it sold before we got it. Like I told you, guy, you stick with old Jack Ross, and you'll really be rollin' in dough." He took a deep breath. "When we get to operating the way we've planned, this measly five bucks'll be chicken feed."

They turned the comer past the police station. Apprehensively Kent scooted down in the seat.

"You don't have to be afraid of those guys, Kent," Jack boasted. "They don't know a thing."

Defiance flamed in Kent's eyes. "I ain't scared of 'em. I ain't scared of nobody!" he snapped.

Jack grinned approvingly. "That's the stuff! That's what I like about you. I need a guy about your age with some real stuff to help me!"

Kent relaxed a little. He had boasted that he wasn't afraid, but deep down inside he was afraid. He was more afraid than he'd ever been in all his life.

"I know you aren't scared," Jack said, "but if it starts to bother you, just relax. The whole deal went off as smooth as silk. The cops don't know a thing."

# CHAPTER 12

# A WAY OUT

Kent Gilbert was working on a model airplane in the kitchen when the mail came the next day. Kay got it and came back to sit down at the kitchen table to look at it. She read a letter from her mother and then picked up the weekly paper.

"Here's something disturbing, Kent," she said. "Did you hear about anyone around town stealing hubcaps, radio antennas, and that sort of thing?"

His young face went ashen, and he dropped the model he was working on.

"How would I hear it?" he demanded belligerently. "I've hardly been out of the house all day."

Kay continued to read. "It says here that the police have been called in to investigate a large number of similar thefts. There's such a pattern that they think the thefts were all committed by the same person or group of persons."

Kent's hands trembled, and he wiped them nervously on his trousers. His lips parted, but he did not speak immediately.

"I don't know why you're readin' all that junk to me," he protested at last. "It don't make no difference to me if someone's stealin' hubcaps off cars. It ain't no skin off my nose. I ain't had nothin' to do with it."

Kay eyed him curiously.

"Nobody said you did," she replied.

It was a minute or two before the boy spoke again. When he did speak, there was a new tone in his voice – something Kay wasn't quite able to understand.

"A minute ago you said you were upset by that story about people stealin' hubcaps," he told her. "What'd you mean by that?"

"Nothing really," she replied, "except that I'm always disturbed when I read about sin. I know what's going to happen to the ones who are doing it."

"Like what?" he asked, trying hard to sound casual and nonchalant.

"For one thing their consciences are going to bother them," she continued. "They can't help it. Especially if this happens to be a gang of boys, which I'm afraid it is.

Kent bristled defensively.

"I don't know why you'd think that. Most boys don't have cars – at least guys my age. What'd they do with hubcaps anyway?"

Kay put the paper aside slowly.

"Kent," she asked, "is there something wrong?"

Belligerence flashed in his eyes.

"What do you mean, 'wrong'?" he demanded.

"You've been acting so strangely ever since I told you about the police investigation of the thefts this week."

"Boy, that's great!" Kent exclaimed. "You read somethin' in the papers, and right away you think I've done it when I ain't even been out of the house alone. That shows what you think of me, I guess."

"I haven't accused you of anything, Kent," she replied. "It's just that you've been acting oddly the last few minutes."

"Who wouldn't act odd?" he shouted. "I get the third degree every time I turn around."

Kay picked up the paper once more and glanced at the account.

"You know that I haven't accused you of anything." She paused. "We'll know who's responsible sooner or later."

Fear leaped to his eyes.

"What do you mean by that?"

"Whoever it is will get caught. They always do."

* * *

That night Kay, Jill, and Kent were just finishing supper when Jill turned cynically to Kay and asked, "Do we have to have Bible reading tonight with Danny gone?"

"We always have our family devotions, Jill," Kay said. "You know that."

Kent jumped to his feet. "I'll get the Bible for you, Kay."

Jill stared questioningly at him.

"Thank you, Kent," Kay said. "It's on the nightstand beside the bed."

In a moment he was back, laying the Bible in front of her. She thanked him, opened it, and began to read.

" 'As it is written, There is none righteous, not even one; there is none who understands, there is none who seeks for God; All have turned aside, together they have become useless; There is none who does good, there is not even one….' "

Kent squirmed uneasily. Those verses were aimed as directly at him as though Kay knew everything that had taken place.

Did she? His heart skipped a beat. *Did she know?*

" '…For all have sinned and fall short of the glory of God; being justified as a gift by His grace through the redemption which is in Christ Jesus;

" 'Whom God displayed publicly as a propitiation in His blood through faith. This was to demonstrate His righteousness, because in the forbearance of God He passed over the sins previously committed; for the demonstration, I say, of His righteousness at the present time, so that He would be just and the justifier of the one who has faith in Jesus.' "

"What does that mean?" Jill broke in.

Kay chose her words carefully.

"It means," she began, "that none of us is good enough

to go to heaven on our own merits – that, regardless of how clean a life we've lived, we're still sinners."

Kent's forehead wrinkled curiously.

Always before he'd felt he wasn't so bad. But now, now! Something died within him.

"But," Kay continued, "God sent the Lord Jesus Christ to shed His blood and suffer on the cross for our sins, so we can be declared just and good, not because of what we've done ourselves, but because of what Christ did for us." She paused, looking from one to the other thoughtfully. "So we can be saved through His righteousness."

Kay continued to explain the meaning of salvation, going over and over it, using different Bible verses to explain it each time.

Jill listened impassively. Kent tried to fight off the impact of Kay's words, but they drove to the very depths of his soul.

"The wages of sin is death! The wages of sin is death!" And there was no doubt that what he had done was sin.

For a moment he felt the weight of all the world on his weary young shoulders. If only he could confess it before God and be rid of it! If only–.

But he could not! If he did, he'd have to go down to the police station and confess to them too! He'd have to squeal on himself and Jack Ross and the rest of the guys. He could never do that!

When Kay finally finished talking and praying, Kent was unusually quiet. Trouble clouded his eyes, and he lingered at the table, toying with his empty glass. The longing to confess still gnawed at him, but grimly he forced his thoughts to other things.

Then Jill came to his rescue. She got to her feet and stomped over to the sink.

"If I have to help with the dishes tonight, I want to get started," she blurted. "I don't want to have to spend all night doin' them." She made it sound as though Kay was the meanest person in the world for expecting her to help with the evening dishes.

Kay ignored her injured tone. "Kent and I will go in the other room, Jill," she said quietly. "You can start on the dishes if you want."

Poutingly, the girl's lower lip curled.

"I don't see why I have to do the dishes," she protested. "I've been studying hard all day. Besides, none of the other girls have to do the dishes at their homes."

Kay smiled pleasantly.

"Here in our home, we all help carry the load," she said.

Kent started for his bedroom, but Kay stopped him.

"I'd like to talk to you for a couple of minutes, Kent," she continued, "if you don't mind."

Reluctantly he crossed to an easy chair and sat down.

"Now what've I done?" Belligerence crept into his voice.

"Nothing."

"I've got a lot of studying to do tonight."

"I just wanted to tell you," Kay went on, "that I was very pleased with your attitude toward our family devotions tonight."

His eyes narrowed. He said nothing.

"But, Kent," she said, "there's something that bothers me a great deal."

"I knew it!" He glared at her. "I knew you'd have something to blast me about."

"I don't want to 'blast' you about anything, Kent." Concern drove the smile from her lips. "I just want to help you if I can."

"I don't need help from nobody."

Kay leaned forward.

"I've been watching you the last few days, Kent," she told him. "You haven't been yourself at all. You haven't been working or studying the way you should. Most of the time you just sit and stare into space."

"I'm all right," he snarled. "There's nothin' wrong with me."

Kay spoke quietly. "Are you in some sort of trouble?"

Kent leaped to his feet. His face was flushed, and anger blazed in his eyes.

"I don't know why you pick on me all the time! I ain't done nothin' wrong! Why don't you get on that Jim Morgan about some of the stuff he does? He ain't as perfect as you think he is."

"We aren't talking about Jim right now," Kay went on. "Danny and I both know that Jim is far from perfect – just as we all are. I'm talking about you, Kent. I don't know what's bothering you, but I know something is."

"Well, there ain't!" he flared. "And you can get off my back about it!"

He stormed into his bedroom and slammed the door, leaving Kay staring sorrowfully after him. *If only he would accept Christ as his Savior,* she thought.

Kent stood in the center of his room, breathing heavily. The color had fled from his face, and his shoulders were trembling. What was the matter with Kay Orlis, anyway? Why did she have to keep nagging at him? Didn't she know a guy liked to be left alone once in a while? He was in enough trouble as it was without having her after him all the time.

Tears clung to his eyelids, and his fists clenched convulsively. The cops were going to catch him for sure! What was he going to do? What could he do?

The desire to yield completely to Christ all but overwhelmed him once more. How he longed to confess his sin to God and then go to Kay and the cops and do the same thing! How he longed to wipe the slate clean!

But he couldn't do that! Not when it would mean sending himself and all the other guys to the reformatory.

In anguish he threw himself on the bed and sobbed silently.

There was only one way out for him, and he wouldn't take it.

www.ingramcontent.com/pod-product-compliance
Lightning Source LLC
Chambersburg PA
CBHW060503300726
48975CB00008B/2618